CACTUS
WEDDING

A TEXAS WINE TRAIL SERIES

≫ BOOK 2 ≪

CACTUS
WEDDING

A TEXAS WINE TRAIL SERIES

⇒ BOOK 2 ⇐

Heather Renée May

MAYDAY PUBLISHING LTD

MayDay Publishing Ltd. Co.
2028 E Ben White Blvd #240-5666
Austin, TX 78741

Cover & Interior Design by the Book Cover Whisperer:
OpenBookDesign.biz

Chapter Illustrations by Victoria Horner
Editing & Proofreading through NYBookEditors
Line/Structural Editing by Megan McKeever
Copyediting by Alison Imbriaco
Headshot/Bio Photos by Abraham Rowe Photography

Library of Congress Control Number: 2022906541

978-1-7377193-3-5 Paperback
978-1-7377193-4-2 eBook

Manufactured in the United States of America

Printing & Distribution by Ingram Spark | Kindle Direct Publishing

FIRST EDITION

And now these three remain: faith, hope and love. But the greatest of these is love.
- **1 Corinthians 13:13**

⇒ Foreword ⇐

This book contains fictional characters, and any resemblance to persons living or dead is purely coincidental. However, the places in this book were real at the time of writing. This book is not meant to be an exhaustive list of wineries or businesses in Fredericksburg and the Texas Hill Country. Rather, the author encourages readers to come visit this beautiful and unique Texas wine country and experience it firsthand. At the back of this book is a listing of all locations highlighted for reference.

Further, this book is not meant to be used as a guide for RV life. There are plenty of resources that are much more comprehensive than this that the author encourages you to explore

One

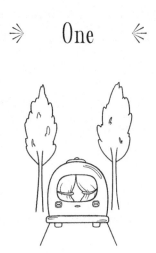

Kate sat at her small dinette and looked out the rounded windows of the Airstream to watch the sunrise just starting to reveal the colors of the day's sky. The RV resort was quiet at dawn, and she listened for the calls of the early morning birds heralding this new day. New Year's Day. She couldn't believe that she was finally getting to see her sister, Lillie. She had hardly slept at all last night, having stayed up chatting until the wee hours with Zach. He and his daughter, Chloe, had decided to spend the holiday together in Marfa, Texas. Kate would have joined them, but she had so much to do to prepare for her sister's return.

She marveled at how quickly things had changed for her. Seemingly overnight.

When she thought back to that day at Pontotoc Vineyard in Fredericksburg, just a few weeks ago, the warm memory filled her heart with joy. Kate had never expected to see Zach again. It was almost too good. Yet, it was true.

She couldn't believe how far she'd come. Had it been only one year since she'd arrived at this RV park, nursing a broken heart, tangled in a difficult divorce? She remembered how tough that time had been, full of questioning herself and wondering where her life would lead. She never would have imagined how meeting Zach that one day at Texas Heritage Vineyard would change her life in so many ways.

Kate smiled to herself at that familiar memory she had revisited many times over the last year. How handsome he had looked in his bright-blue vest. How delightful their conversation had been. Zach was taking a break from his medical practice in the Northeast to scout for a winery to invest in. They had decided to pal around that week to enjoy tastings together. As the wine flowed, so had their conversations. Kate remembered how they danced together at Hye Meadow Winery, their cheeks pressing gently against each other: a perfect fit. Then a phone call had pulled him back to the Northeast, leaving Kate reeling in the dust of his departure. They had chosen not to share each other's contact information as it would be too complicated.

Kate believed in fate, but she had never truly thought they would meet again.

She looked out the windows and squeezed her warm mug of coffee in gratitude. So many gifts. What had seemed to take forever now seemed to all be happening in an instant. The tide had turned.

Seeing Zach again was nearly as unbeliev-able as the fact that her sister was flying across the world to come home. Kate wasn't sure why Lillie was coming back now and wondered at her plans. As far as she knew, Lillie was staying for just six days with her. After?

Lillie hadn't given her a definitive answer. She took a deep breath in to try and settle her anxiety. Kate felt her season of drought was over, which was both exciting and scary. She wasn't yet sure how she would navigate the incoming waves.

Kate remembered the last time she saw Lil-lie. They had just left the hospice room and had stepped outside to breathe fresh air and accept their new reality of loss. They had held each other, although all their tears had been shed and there were no more words. Just that feeling of empty space where their mother once fit.

The next day, Lillie left for France. That was three years ago.

Kate had felt abandoned by Lillie's departure and overwhelmed by all the details with regard to planning their mother's burial. Writing the ten lines of their mother's obituary might have been the hardest task Kate had ever taken on. Summing her mother's life up in a short paragraph seemed to devalue the enormous impact she'd had on their lives. The hole she had left in their hearts.

Kate sighed at the memory of those feelings and then took another sip from her mug. It was time for a new start. She truly hoped she and her sister could bridge the seven-year gap in their ages and their time apart. Lillie had sounded so good, and Kate reminded herself to not mother her. To just be her sister and let Lillie be the grown woman she had become. This wasn't easy for Kate, and she prayed she would have guidance.

She spied Sirius twinkling at her, low on the horizon as the morning colors gradually grew brighter. *Lord, let us have that homecoming I've been dreaming about.*

⇒ Two ⇐

Lillie adjusted herself against the uncomfort-able metal seat at Charles de Gaulle Airport. The magnificent sounds of the jet engines rumbled beyond the thickly paned glass as the intercom overhead pierced the hum of multiple conversations with informational messages in French. She glanced up at the monitor to see that boarding would begin in ten minutes. Taking a deep breath, she opened her bottle of water and let the cool, clean fluid trickle down her throat. Her red fiddle case sat in the vacant chair next to her, and she nudged it as she returned the bottle to her leather knapsack. The rest of her belongings, including her guitar, she assumed were being safely stowed into the belly of the 787.

It had been a long time since Lillie had seen her sister, Kate. When their mother finally gave up her fight against cancer, Lillie had been overwhelmed by the loss. She had chosen to immediately head out on tour with her band to France. The relentless tour schedule, travel, and scenery distracted her so that she could subconsciously work out her feelings over time. Being on the other side of the "pond" gave her a sense of having a buffer. She was in a different world. A place filled with delicious bread, pastries, and cheese. A foreign language that Lillie became fully immersed in, as though diving into the deep blue waters and emerging as another shade of herself.

Now, it was New Year's Day. A year that was

already surprising her with change. Here she was, boarding a plane to travel back. In a matter of hours, she would return to the States to assume her American identity. Lillie wasn't sure how she felt about this. Would she be a foreigner in her birth country? What would it be like to see Kate again? It wasn't just the time away or the geographical distance. Coming back home was like opening Pandora's box. She worried about the feelings that might come up. Those feelings she had stuffed deep down when she left. Lillie nervously fingered the straps on her knapsack, rubbing the smooth worn leather.

She pulled out a paperback and ran her fingers over the beautiful cover, amazed that her sister had done it again. A *New York Times* best-selling novel in the top ten for the last four weeks. She marveled and at the same time felt a slight tinge of jealousy. It sometimes seemed to her that Kate had a way of being really good at whatever she did. That it came easy for her.

Lillie knew that Kate had divorced David, but she still wasn't sure why. They had seemed so happy and perfect. Maybe a little too perfect?

Austin, Texas. Well, that was different. She was relieved that she wasn't flying all the way back to the Pacific Northwest. Lillie felt ready to see her sister but not as ready to return to her childhood landscape. She shivered at the thought of the gray blanket that covered the Northwest this time of year. The wet cold that penetrated no matter how many layers you wore.

No. Lillie was relieved to be landing in a place of sunshine and warmth. She wanted to see what Kate's life was like now. The fact that she was living full time in an Airstream sounded so romantic. Kate had told Lillie about this new love interest, Zach. Did he seem too good to be true? A doctor moving to a small town in Texas to open a winery and tasting room? It sounded like a plot right out of one of her sister's books. Lillie was looking forward to visiting this German town—Fredericksburg—that she'd read about. She wanted to see and experience the Texas wine trail for herself.

An announcement overhead interrupted her thoughts, and she looked up to see people queuing to board the plane. She tucked the book away and stood up, stretching, then scanned the room to take in one last breath of this place. She would miss seeing French signs as the norm. She would miss the safety blanket this country had been for her. Reluctantly, Lillie grabbed her case and knapsack and made her way to line up with the boarding passengers, her iPhone lit with the boarding code, ready to scan. It was time to go home, and Lillie hoped she was ready.

Three

Kate was seated in her Durango with the engine humming, waiting curbside at Austin-Bergstrom International Airport. She fidgeted in her seat and peered through her windows to the glass doors, anxious for a glance of her dear sister. It was a typical day in Austin for this time of year: just cold enough to warrant a lightweight sweater but with warm sunrays lighting up the brown cement surfaces of the building.

Just then, she caught the reflection of a bright-red case poking up and saw Lillie push through the glass doors with her black guitar case in front and her fiddle case strapped to her back. Her dark hair was cut in a chic bob, and she was wearing a black jeans jacket with a beautiful silk scarf wrapped around her delicate neck. Lillie.

Kate opened her door and waved to her as she went around the back of the SUV to open the door for her bags. In a few short steps, they bridged the gap.

"You made it!" Kate exclaimed, as Lillie smiled back. "Happy New Year!" They tried to hug and realized it was futile with the luggage.

"Let me grab this," Kate said as she took the guitar case and duffel, while Lillie maneuvered out of the straps on her fiddle case.

Once it was safely stowed on top, Kate turned to hug her. She pulled her little sister against her bosom and felt a sense of peace and relief wash over her. Finally, they were back together. She knew they had many things to sort out, but they would hopefully have time for that over the next few days. Now, she was just grateful to have her close.

They pulled away with teary eyes and then hurried into the Durango to pull out of the pick-up zone so other travelers could also fetch their loved ones.

"I can't believe you're here!" Kate exclaimed as she merged into traffic.

"Seriously, me too. It's been forever since I was in the States." Lillie slowly exhaled.

"How was your flight?" Kate asked as she turned on a blinker.

"It was actually good. Not as long as I expected, what with the jet stream and all," Lillie said. "I really enjoyed just having time to rest and read. You know, I'm reading this fabulous book about the Texas wine trail..." She smirked at Kate, and they laughed together.

"Oh my gosh, can you even believe that this happened?" Kate asked her sister. "I mean, I had no idea whether I could write another book, let alone a novel, but apparently fiction is my genre." She added quickly, "And obviously, wine."

They laughed together harmoniously, the way sisters do.

"Were you able to get me a reservation in the vintage trailer?" Lillie asked.

"Yes! I have it all set up for you. I even did a little grocery shopping, so you'd have coffee, tea, creamer, and cheese." Kate looked at her sideways for a second. "Of course, it won't be nearly as good as what you had in France."

"That's fine, sis. I mean, I can rough it for a little while," Lillie joked as she adjusted her seat belt.

Kate carefully merged onto 71, and they headed northwest, away from Austin, toward the Hill Country and Spicewood. She felt a bit self-conscious, as though she was trying too hard to please her sister, but she couldn't help it. She wanted so very badly for this trip to go well.

As Kate navigated the dense traffic, Lillie filled in the conversation gaps with stories from her tour abroad.

"Once, we were scheduled to play in this tiny bar tucked away underneath this bridge in Paris," Lillie explained. "But there wasn't enough room for us all to fit in the corner, so the owner said with a wave of his arms, *'Mais! Sur la table!'*" Lillie imitated the owner with a flick of her head and wrist. "So we ended up standing on the tables and chairs to play over the crowd!" Kate joined her in laughter, thinking how she missed the tinkle of notes in her sister's voice.

"Were you mostly playing gigs in Paris?" Kate asked.

"We had a regular gig in the Marais, but we also played all over. From Tourcoing to Toulouse. Marseille. Bordeaux. Oh! There was this lovely little place in La Rochelle we got to stay at," Lillie continued. "It's amazing. You can still see the scars from the Allied occupation."

Kate shook her head sadly as she kept her eyes on the Tesla's brake lights in front of her.

Lillie continued, "Really, throughout all of France, there are still remnants. I find it incredible that these cities are now thriving after so much destruction."

Kate stopped at the light and took the opportunity to turn to her sister. Lillie's dark bangs accented her beautiful brown eyes, and the sunlight highlighted her fair skin, illuminating her face. Precious.

"It just goes to show that we truly are a resilient human race. Even in the most difficult hardship, we can rise again," Lillie said.

Kate turned her head back as the light changed, and she accelerated forward. She wondered if that was true. Would they be able to rise again after their loss?

"I think the thing I will miss the most is the bread. There is something different about French bread. Something in the flour and yeast. I have never tasted baguettes here in the States that even come close," Lillie said her tone lighter.

"Well, you're in Texas now. You'll be trading in baguettes for tortillas," Kate laughed. "I'll make you a taco lover yet."

Lillie smirked and accepted the challenge. "I'm willing to give anything a try once."

Just then, Kate veered to the right, and the road began to open up as they pulled farther away from Austin and toward the Hill Country. The dense buildings on the sides of the road became more intermittent, and the browns and muted greens of the land became more prominent.

Lillie looked out her window and watched the landscape as it emerged into view. A few proud oak trees dotted an open field, and cattle grazed in their shade. The road continued to wind around, and before long the elevation changed to reveal trees and houses that seemed to blanket the hills.

"Wow, this is so different. It's really beautiful in a sort of desert-like way," Lillie pondered aloud.

"Yeah, it takes a little getting used to," Kate said. "At first, I wasn't sure I would like the dry, prickliness of it." She glanced to the side. "But the big sky gets me every time. Just wait till you see tonight's stars."

Lillie smiled as she took it all in—the rugged stones, paddle cactuses, and rolling hills.

Kate flicked her blinker on and then turned off Highway 71 and onto a smaller two-lane paved road that wound more tightly through the scrub oaks. With each turn, she had to slow down in order to stay in her lane.

For Lillie, each mile took them farther into the wildness. Every bend seemed to produce

a unique view, with old oak branches providing a canopy over their vehicle. They wound
around and then descended before driving up
again and over another hill, where they turned
sharply onto a road to skirt the edge of another,
larger hill.

She watched the scenery open up again
as they drove along this vista of sky and hills
stretching infinitely. She saw a sign for the
Stone House Vineyard, and then they passed
a golf course.

Before long, Kate slowed down, and Lillie
saw the red lit sign for Open Air RV Resorts.
Just like in the book. She giggled in delight and
anticipation as she saw fiction become reality
before her eyes.

Kate pulled in, observing the five-mile-an-
hour speed limit. They drove past the pond and
then the main office, which looked like a sweet
cabin built with jagged chunks of limestone.

Kate waved as she rolled past a few dog walkers, and Lillie watched as the shiny metal tubes appeared just past the pool area.

She squealed in excitement. "Which one?"

Kate laughed as she pulled in front of the silver 1955 Spartan skirted with peach paint. "Meet Lucille!"

Lillie hardly let her pull to a stop before jumping out of the Durango and taking a look for herself. "She's gorgeous!" she exclaimed and stepped up to the deck to peer into the shiny windows. "Retro, chic!"

"Well, she's yours for the week," Kate said as she stepped past her sister and put a key in the door to let her in.

Once inside, Lillie took in the open space. The gray sofa against one end. The wooden counters with lime-green painted doors. The white-tiled backsplash behind the sink.

"This is where you wrote your book?" she asked Kate.

"Well, unfortunately, that trailer was unavailable. It's right next door, though. And anyway, the only difference is that this one doesn't have the dinette," Kate said. "But I figured you'd be coming to eat at my trailer most of the time anyway."

Lillie nodded in agreement. "I can't wait to see your Airstream too!" She continued to walk through the trailer and saw the bunk beds and the bathroom, before finally ending up at the back where the full bed beckoned. She suddenly felt the weight of the trip and the time change.

"I may want to take a little nap, if that's OK?" Lillie asked.

"Of course!" Kate said. "Let's grab your things, and you just do whatever you need to do to get settled in."

They made their way to the front of the trailer and stepped out onto the patio, which was shaded by a canvas awning gently billowing in the breeze.

Once they'd brought her luggage and instruments inside, Kate turned to give her sister another hug. "I'm so glad you are here, Lillie," she breathed out.

Lillie pulled away before saying, "Me too."

"There's some snacks and water in the fridge. Just text me when you are up and about. I have a simple dinner planned at my campsite, and we can just take it easy tonight." Kate stalled before stepping outside the trailer and finally closing the door behind her.

She got back in her Durango and pulled out slowly to make her way to the end of the park and back to her own home. Kate breathed out relief. Home.

Lillie was finally home.

Four

"So how does it feel?" Zach asked her.

Kate listened to his deep voice on the other end of her phone. "Between talking with you and having my sister here, I am so full I can honestly burst," she stated.

"Kate, that's awesome. As much as I want to spend more time with you, I think that we couldn't have planned this better. You needed one-on-one time with your sister."

"Like we planned this?" They both chuckled

into the phone. "But you're right. And I'm glad you get to spend more time with Chloe."

"It's been so much fun here with her, and she's getting really good at her photography," he said.

It was all perfectly unplanned. After meeting a year ago on the Texas wine trail, they had enjoyed tastings and conversation for a week. Zach was already divorced and scouting for a winery to invest in. His daughter, Chloe, was getting ready to graduate and looking at her options for college. Zach had hoped she would attend his alma mater, UT. Then Chloe had an accident, and he had to suddenly leave. Kate and Zach hadn't talked again until they saw each other at Pontotoc Weingarten a few weeks ago. Without knowing it, they had ended up in the same place at the same time a year later. Chloe got into UT. Zach relocated to Austin to help her adjust and find investors for his winery. Kate embraced full-time RV living and made the Hill

Country her home to work on her next novel. It was pretty unbelievable.

Kate was hopeful for the first time in years. She wasn't sure how their relationship would work. He was renting an apartment with Chloe an hour away in Austin and then splitting his time in Fredericksburg, which added another half hour of travel time. They were close, but just far enough apart to make it a bit difficult to visit on a regular basis. So far, they'd only been able to carve out a few dinners before the holidays came and he left with Chloe for East Texas.

Kate hoped she would have more time in the future to get to know Chloe. She wanted her to be comfortable, especially if the relationship was going to last.

"Well, for sure I want to see what she's been shooting," Kate said. "But I would very much like to spend more one-on-one time with her father."

Zach cleared his throat. "I can't wait to see you and kiss you again."

Kate felt a tingling all through her body. As if he were whispering right in her ear.

"I miss your lips...and touch..." she trailed off as they both sighed heavily into the phone.

"Soon."

"Yes."

The phone was silent with the fullness of their desire before they reluctantly rang off.

It was nearly five, and Kate double-checked her phone for a text from Lillie. The cabin of her Bambi Airstream was filled with the delicious scent of chili. She had decided to make a Texas favorite in the Crock-Pot for Lillie's return. She had even baked homemade corn bread in the cast-iron skillet and couldn't wait to have a hot piece dripping with butter and honey. She lifted the top of the pot and stirred the chili. It was perfectly done and just waiting for her guest.

Her phone finally dinged.

"Up. Where am I? LOL"

Kate laughed and then typed back: "Heaven. I'll be right there."

She stepped out of her trailer, walked briskly up the road to Lucille, and met Lillie outside the bright trailer.

"Did you sleep OK?" Kate asked.

"Oh my gosh, yes. I mean, like the dead," Lillie responded as she fell into step with her sister and they made their way back up the road.

Lillie regarded all the different types of trailers and RVs lined up in rows throughout the park.

"Wow, this is so cool to see up close. RV life isn't as popular in France as it apparently is here."

"Everything is bigger in Texas, but in general RV living has become really big all over the States," Kate boasted. "Part of the whole simple-living trend, it's become a way for folks to afford a home and also travel. And now with

Wi-Fi everywhere, there's so many more folks working remotely too."

Lillie nodded as she took in a Tiffin motorhome next to an R-Pod travel trailer. "There's just so many types. How did you choose yours?"

"Airstreams just have this iconic feel. And I love how cozy and secure I feel in mine," Kate said as they rounded the bend and hers came into view. "Here she is!" she exclaimed.

"Oh my gosh! She's even cuter in person!" Lillie squealed as she got closer. She walked all around the outside and said, delighted, *"Un œuf d'argent!"* Then translated, "A perfect silver egg!"

Kate grinned and beckoned her inside.

At the tiny doorway, Lillie paused to take in the smells from the chili and the cute camper hooks where Kate had her jackets and bags hung. She stepped up and into the trailer, her eyes wide.

"Sis, this is *so* adorable!" she said. "And what the heck is that delicious smell?"

"Texas chili and corn bread," Kate answered. "Figured you'd want some comfort food after the long flight, and I wanted to give your taste buds a kick start."

Kate took a deep breath and let it out. *Sis.* It felt so good to be called that again.

She showed Lillie around her small home. She pointed out all the features—places for storage, the wet bath, and the full-size bed with the star-gazing window.

"This is my favorite spot in the trailer," Kate said as she pointed at the window. "I can lie in bed and see the stars as they shine at night, just like those glow-in-the-dark stars we used to have on our bedroom ceiling as kids. Remember?" she asked.

Lillie nodded absently, as though her mind had gone to another place for a moment, before finally responding, "I don't remember those, but I can imagine."

They turned around to the front of the

trailer and settled into the tiny dinette with the wraparound windows facing the park.

"I mean, this is super tiny from the outside, but it's surprisingly big and homey inside," Lillie said.

"I didn't want anything much bigger. I needed to be able to tow it with my Durango, and I like that it's easy to fit anywhere." She pointed to the large fifth wheels across the way. "It's great to have all that space and storage, but sometimes it can be difficult to drive or find a place to park."

Kate looked back at Lillie. "I also love that this *feels* like I'm camping, rather than living in a house."

Lillie nodded in agreement. "I'm just amazed that you have everything you need."

"You'd be surprised how many things we think we *need* but then find we can live without," Kate replied.

Kate got up and opened up the top cabinet door to pull out two tan bowls. "Ready to eat?" she asked Lillie as she began to ladle the steaming chili.

"*Mais, oui!*" Lillie smiled.

Kate retrieved butter and a bag of shredded cheddar cheese from the fridge. Then she put everything out on the table. She sliced the corn bread up in the skillet and placed a pie-shaped piece on a smaller plate for Lillie.

They sat down and got comfortable. Bowing her head, Kate said, "Lord, thank you for bringing Lillie home safe and for blessing our bodies with this food. Amen."

Lillie took a bite and declared. "Oh, wow, sis. I forgot how darn good American food is."

Kate beamed and took a bite herself, delighting in the texture and spicy flavor that enveloped her palate. Between spoonfuls, Kate and Lillie continued catching up.

"How are you doing now?" Lillie asked before breaking off another piece of corn bread. "I mean, without David?"

Kate swallowed hard as she thought about how to answer this. Her ex-husband was a famous documentary filmmaker and her idol. She had sought him out to be a mentor, but they ended up falling in love and marrying with breathtaking speed. Soon after, Kate realized she may have made a mistake, but it was too late: she'd been sucked into his world of glamour and notoriety. When she found love notes from supposed "friends" tucked into his luggage while he was away on location, she knew she had to trust her gut. It had been the hardest decision to leave him—and now, in hindsight, probably the best.

"I'm doing good," she replied to her younger sister. "It was tough at first, making the choice to leave and disappointing so many people. But

I never would have realized my true dream of writing a novel if I'd stayed." She shrugged before looking back at Lillie. "Things happen the way they should."

"*C'est la vie*," Lillie replied. "You just seemed so happy together, traveling around the country, working on his films."

"That was just it, though: it was always about his work. I was never given the opportunity to focus on my writing the way I thought I would." Kate thought for a moment. "In fact, he really discouraged my dreams. Said we were 'one' now and his life was mine. But that really just meant that he wanted everything to be about him." She fingered her spoon before adding, "He was terrified to not be in the spotlight. To no longer be relevant."

"For someone so famous and talented, it is surprising that he was so insecure, no?" Lillie took another spoonful of chili.

"It's really sad." Kate just nodded.

"Do you miss him?" Lillie pointedly asked her.

"A year ago, I would have said yes. Now? I just wish the best for him, and I am truly grateful to have the life I live." Kate looked out the window. "I mean, it may seem sort of strange that a grown woman in her forties would choose to live inside a small metal trailer hardly the size of one of my closets back in Charleston." She grinned at Lillie. "I wouldn't trade it for the world."

"I think you are very brave." Lillie said, and they held each other's gaze for a moment.

"Oh! I almost forgot," Kate exclaimed as she got up from the dinette and grabbed a bottle of Barbera from Hye Meadow Winery and two glasses. "How could I serve you a Texas meal without the Hill Country wine to go with it?"

Lillie grinned but then looked a little uncomfortable. Kate wasn't sure why, but as she began pouring a glass, Lillie shook her head and said, "I'm OK."

Kate was taken aback a bit. "Wait, how can you live in France all this time and not want wine? Trust me, Texas wine is really good."

"No, no. It's not that." Lillie paused awkwardly. "It's just that I am taking a break from drinking for a bit."

Kate looked at her suspiciously, then said, "Well, OK. More for me." She finished pouring her glass and offered to fill up Lillie's water glass.

"So, you haven't told me why you are back?" Kate asked as the rich red washed over her palate.

Lillie fidgeted on the dinette bench. "Well, my work visa ran out, and I thought it would be a good time to take a break from touring and maybe deal with some loose ends back in the Northwest."

"You know Mom's house sold, right?" Kate asked her sister.

"Yes. Thanks for sending me the check." Lillie said in a way that felt to Kate as though she resented her being in charge.

"It wasn't much after paying off her medical bills, but at least it was something," Kate said and swallowed hard.

Lillie looked out the window absently, and Kate wondered if they had already reached that point in their visit where they would settle back into old roles—her making decisions, and Lillie avoiding. Kate thought about how quickly the past catches up.

"Before I left, I put my things in storage, and I want to go back to Port Angeles to get them out," Lillie said.

"Are you planning to stay in the Northwest?" Kate asked her sister.

"I don't know. Maybe?" Lillie said exasperated. "I just need some time to figure things out."

Kate knew she needed to back off. She knew

not to press her sister when she got like this. Lillie would reveal her intentions when she was ready.

They would have almost a week together, and Kate didn't want to mess it up by digging too deep on the first day. She just hoped that Lillie would open up eventually.

Trust takes time, and they had a lot of time to catch up on to gain that back.

"How about tomorrow we head to Fredericksburg and you can meet Zach?" Kate asked hoping to break the tension.

"Yes! I really want to see this place you've described so well in your book." Lillie brightened and the air grew lighter between them again. "Tell me, is his tasting room open yet?"

"Not yet. He hopes to open this spring, in time to capitalize on all the tourists who come for bluebonnet season." Kate took another sip of wine.

"So, you've only been together now for a few weeks, right?" Lillie probed, relieved to take the pressure off herself.

"Yes." Kate fingered the rim of her glass.

"How's that going?" Lillie asked.

"Good, so far." Kate looked up at her. "We picked right back up where we left off, and he's just amazing in so many ways," she trailed off.

"But?"

"Well, it's a bit tricky with the distance. Trying to coordinate dates between his time with Chloe, the winery, and the travel time..." She hesitated, then added, "It's just been a bit of a challenge."

"So, why don't you move closer to him?" Lillie asked.

Kate immediately felt her defenses go up. "No."

She thought about her move from New York to Charleston after marrying David and how much she lost of herself in that process. She had promised herself not to do that again.

Kate looked at her sister. "I love it here. Besides, it's too soon."

"I'm sure you'll figure out how to be together when the time's right," Lillie said and smiled encouragingly at her sister.

"There's no rush." She finished her glass of wine and got up to put their empty bowls in the sink.

"Absolutely," Lillie said with a yawn.

"Listen, let's get you back to your trailer, and we can continue this in the morning," Kate said.

"Yeah, I could definitely use a good night's sleep."

They walked back up the road together, and Kate pointed out the stars that had just begun to shine brightly above them.

"Wow," Lillie breathed. "It's like you said, truly magical."

Kate smiled as she hugged her sister close and then watched Lillie let herself into the trailer. It was a complicated start already, but she hoped that they would settle into a more comfortable rhythm over the next few days.

As Kate walked back to her home, she looked up at the stars and saw one shining brighter than the others. On that one, she made the wish that she and her sister would find common ground again. That their future would be guided by the stars and be just as magical.

⇛ Five ⇚

"Well, it's about time you called!" Caroline practically yelled into the phone. "I've been waiting for an update. Tell me, how's Lillie?" She stopped short, coming up for air.

Kate grinned at the lovely sound of her dear friend's voice. Caroline had been her friend—and more like family—for years. She had been a champion for Kate through the divorce and was the reason she had rented the Airstream trailer in the Hill Country to begin with. Kate had just separated from her ex and was up against the deadline for her third book. With Caroline's prompting, she ended up renting the trailer, writing her book, and subsequently meeting Zach.

"She looks really good," Kate said.

"And?" Caroline prodded.

"Well, it's been a little awkward getting back in sync. She's pretty guarded and hasn't yet told me really why she's back. Just some vague need to 'deal with loose ends.'" Kate paused, searching for words to explain her uneasiness.

"Sisters are tough." Caroline said into the phone. "I thank my lucky stars every day that I have a big brother. He watched out for me but also didn't feel the need to compete."

"You know that we've always struggled, particularly with the age difference. It's just hard for me to not need to take care of her in some way," Kate said.

"I'm sure she appreciates and resents the hell out of that," Caroline snickered.

"True." Kate laughed. "It really has been great to be close again, though. We've sort of tap-danced around the issue of our mother's death." Kate told her about how they had chili and that she had shared about her divorce last year. "It was strange going back into that again. It feels like ancient history for me, but since she wasn't here, it was news to her."

"Isn't that funny? How you can be out of touch with someone and your lives will move forward on different paths, but then when you meet up again, you end up right back where you left off?" Caroline took a breath before asking, "Was it hard to talk about?"

Kate shook her head even though Caroline couldn't see her. "No. Actually, it felt good to talk about it and finally feel free from the grief. As if I was looking at it in the rearview mirror."

"Good. As it should be," Caroline stated.

"We're planning to head to Fredericksburg today and grab brunch before meeting up with Zach." Kate grinned.

"Wonderful! How is our favorite Dr. Wine?" Caroline asked.

"Oh, he's doing great. He enjoyed the holidays with Chloe in Marfa," Kate said. "I still can't believe it. It's like everything changed overnight. It feels good, though."

Caroline cooed, "Oh, gurrl, I told you that when it's right, it can feel seamless. Which can be unnerving if you are used to bumps in the road."

Kate laughed. "Yeah, more like potholes. I'm still getting used to talking with him on a regular basis. He's really good about keeping in touch even though he's been so busy."

"I hope you two get some quality alone time together soon," Caroline said.

"This week is all about Lillie, but then hope-fully we'll be able to carve out more time." Even as she spoke, Kate wondered how she would feel suddenly having to share her time with someone else on a regular basis. Aloud, she only said, "For now, we're still getting to know each other."

"Take your time," Caroline advised before saying she needed to ring off to make the kids breakfast. "Keep me posted, darlin'. And be sure to tell that sister of yours hello and that she owes me a phone call!"

"Will do, love!"

With that, Kate finished her cup of coffee and sent a text off to her sister.

"Let me know when you are ready to head to Fredericksburg. Xo"

A few seconds later, a ping.

"I'm up. Enjoying coffee now, and I'll be ready in about an hour!"

Kate smiled and felt that familiar warmth spread through her chest at having her sister so close. There's something about family, she thought, that no matter how far apart you've been, once you are near, you feel that deep bond of connection. It's a different kind of knowing— something that withstands the test of time.

Six

The downtown streets of Fredericksburg still displayed their holiday decorations. Wreaths and boughs of green with bright-red ribbons adorned the buildings and outposts, and a huge white banner that hung high above the main street announced, "175th Anniversary." Founded in 1846, the German settlement had withstood the tests of time, weather, and culture. Maintaining German traditions while assimilating into American and, in particular, Texan

ways, Fredericksburg elegantly and proudly
balanced both.

Kate and Lillie marveled at all the shops.
"It's much larger than I expected," Lillie said,
peering into the storefront windows as they
walked the strip. "I love how old these buildings are! I mean, I am used to this in France,
but you don't think that this is something you
would find in Texas."

"It really is something special." Kate grinned,
then wrapped her arm in her sister's and pulled
her forward.

"Up ahead is where I thought we'd stop for a
bite to eat. At Vaudeville." She pointed to a grand
white two-story porch up the block. As they approached, the details became more prominent.
The ball-and-stick spandrels, gingerbread-trim
arches, and gas lanterns gave them both a sense
of the town's Victorian history.

They stepped through the beautifully
carved, white wooden doors and into seemingly

another world. Modern met antique, and the unique decor delighted them at every turn. One of the few brick-only buildings in downtown Fredericksburg, the interior showcased the warmth of the brick while adding more modern touches with white wooden bookshelves and mixed-media metal and wood tables and chairs. Each story of the building had a different vibe. The top, a showroom for art and events. The main floor was set up to display artwork, fine leather goods, jewelry, books, and other gifts. The bistro was down beautiful old wooden stairs with iron railings. They found a seat on either side of a marble bistro table, with Kate sitting in the chair and Lillie making herself comfortable on the cushioned black-leather bench opposite.

"This used to be a speakeasy," Kate said as they both took in the recessed shelving, lit to display fine art and decor.

"The dish of the day is duck confit, with Dijon potatoes and a red raspberry gastrique," the waitress said as she poured them chilled tap water out of a glass bottle.

"That sounds delicious. I'll do that, please, and a glass of the Augusta white wine," Kate said.

"Same for me, except I'll just have water," Lillie said as the waitress took their menus and walked away.

Kate eyed Lillie for a moment and had that sense in her gut that her sister wasn't telling her something.

The waitress delivered the glass of wine, and Kate took a sip before looking up at her sister. "So, what are your plans?"

Lillie took a deep breath and settled into the bench a little more before answering. "Well, I think I'll head back to Port Angeles and maybe see about getting a steady gig at Castaways."

"I remember the owners really liked you there." Kate paused, then asked, "What happened with your band in France?"

Lillie turned her gaze away for a moment,

"Oh, it was time for a change." She looked up as Kate encouraged her to continue with her eyes.

"We were on tour for so long, and honestly I needed the break." Lillie stated as she shrugged her shoulders. "Matthieu, our bass player, needed to spend time with his family in Provence, and Paul was having a hard time committing to the gigs." She looked up at Kate. "I really got tired of being the one in charge of everything. The bookings, the overnights, the food budget." She grimaced. "I started to feel like the band mom, instead of the artist."

Kate nodded in agreement. She remembered how her role with David quickly evolved from wife to his assistant as she planned his complicated traveling schedule. "I can definitely understand how organizing others would become exhausting really quick."

"Let's just say that the life of a touring musician sounds romantic but quickly loses its appeal." Lillie said finally.

The waitress brought their plates, and they savored each bite of the meal in silence, with the ambient music playing softly through their thoughts.

"I was thinking we could go to the beach for an overnight if you were interested?" Kate asked.

"Ooh, that would be lovely. I miss the water. My time in Biarritz was one of my favorites on tour," Lillie said.

"Perfect. We can head out early tomorrow and be at Port Aransas by noon." Kate beamed. "You'll love it. I'll hitch up the camper, and we can park right on the beach and wake up to the ocean out our front door."

"That sounds amazing." Lillie smiled. "What a cool life you have created for yourself with this camper."

"It is. I don't know why I didn't do this before. I really love trailer life."

The waitress brought the check, and Kate snatched it up. "My treat!"

"Thanks, sis." Lillie laughed. "So, when am I going to meet Dr. Wine?"

"Now!" Kate grinned and felt that tingle in her chest as she thought of seeing Zach again. "He said he'd be at the new tasting room this afternoon. It's not far from here." Kate stood up and Lillie maneuvered herself off the bench to follow.

They made their way out the front door and back onto Main Street. It wasn't busy enough to feel crowded, as it was early in the week, and Kate loved the fact that they could stroll leisurely down the sidewalks and actually see all the storefronts.

"Every weekend this street gets jam-packed with tourists," she told Lillie. "I love coming when it's quieter like this."

Lillie nodded as she took in all the different window displays and decorations. "They really like Christmas here, don't they?"

"Yes. It's one of the things that drew me to

this place. The Victorian Christmas charm—and the delicious wine!"

They soon arrived at another transom, and Lillie peered through the showroom window that had "WW" etched elegantly in the glass.

Kate felt giddy as she opened up the heavy wooden door and they stepped inside the empty room.

"Hello?" Kate sang.

"Coming!" She heard his deep voice from the backroom and grinned with delight.

Lillie walked around the open room and took in all the beautiful oak tables and chairs. "This is gorgeous!" she exclaimed to Kate.

Kate was about to respond when Zach appeared. "There you are!" he said to her as he pulled her into a warm hug. He kissed her cheek softly before turning to Lillie. "And you must be the famous musician sister?" He smiled and offered his hand.

Lillie grinned and shook his right back.

"Well, infamous, really. I should think you are much more famous, being Dr. Wine and all." She grinned at him, and they all chuckled.

"Touché," he said, then looked back at Kate. "What do you think?"

"Zach, it's really beautiful. You've gotten so much done since I last visited. Do you think you'll be able to open as expected?" Kate asked.

"As long as there are no hiccups, we'll be in business." He turned to some boxes behind him. "I do have some bottles from local wineries. If you'd like, I can open one to taste?"

"Yes, please!" Kate said as she continued to walk around the room, taking in all the changes.

"Make yourselves comfortable," he said, then moved behind the bar and pulled a bottle out of a box.

The sisters settled in a spot where they could look out through the storefront windows to see foot traffic picking up outside.

Zach placed wine glasses in front of Lillie

and Kate. "Just water for me, if that's OK?" Lillie quickly said, and Zach raised his eyebrows in a question to Kate before he went to the bar for a bottle of water and filled up her glass with the clear liquid.

He then poured Kate a generous glass of a deep red. "Try this," he said as he lifted his own glass and made a toast. "To new beginnings and family." They clinked glasses together.

Kate swirled the glass, then took a sip. It was a bright, rich blend of Sangiovese and something she couldn't quite put her finger on. The raspberry notes gave way to clove and then a hint of peppercorn before the tannins tingled the sides of her mouth with delightful finish.

"Oh, this is really good!" she exclaimed and watched his face light up.

"Right? This is one of my favorite blends from Becker Vineyards," he said, savoring a sip himself.

"What is the blend?" Kate asked Zach.

"It's a blend of Sangiovese, Tempranillo, and Mourvèdre from the High Plains," he said with pride.

"This seems like a great everyday wine," Kate stated.

"Exactly. Something that is rich and approachable." He nodded to her over his glass.

Kate raised her glass to him and said, "Cheers." They clinked glasses and took another long sip.

"So, what do you all have planned for the week?" Zach asked.

Kate told him about their plans to head to Port Aransas for an overnight, then added, "We should plan for dinner before Lillie leaves. Maybe with Chloe?"

"Absolutely. Let's do Otto's?" Zach asked Kate.

"Perfect." She grinned and turned to Lillie. "You'll love their duck schnitzel!"

"What about you?" she asked as she turned back to Zach.

"I'm meeting our growers in the High Plains this week to check on our vines. My business partner Dennis and I will fly out to Lubbock and back the same day with the guys from William Chris Vineyards," he replied, then took the last sip out of his glass.

"That's so exciting. Someday I'd love to visit those vineyards too," Kate said before finishing hers as well.

"Absolutely. I'd love to take you. It's such a different terroir than here in the Hill Country, and the growers are really friendly and knowledgeable."

"We should probably get out of your hair and let you get back to it," Kate said as she turned to Lillie. "Are you ready to do a little shopping before heading back to Spicewood?"

Lillie smiled. "Yes, I am feeling a nap may be in order soon, too, after that delicious brunch."

Zach came around the bar and hugged

Lillie. "It's really wonderful to meet you. Welcome back!"

He then turned to Kate and drew her in close. "And you." He grinned at her, and Kate could feel her heartbeat skip. "I've been away from you for far too long." he whispered in her ear as he pulled her close and then placed his lips gently and firmly on hers. She delighted in the embrace, feeling warmth throughout her entire body as his lips felt electric on hers.

After a moment that felt way too short, she said, "How does that feel so incredible every time?"

Zach grinned and gently stroked her cheek. "When it's right, it's right." He kissed her once more as if to prove his point, then pulled away.

"OK, you two! Go have fun, and I'll get back to work here," he said.

They both laughed and waved goodbye before walking out through the front doors. Once they were down the block a bit, Lillie exclaimed, "Oh my gosh, sis, he is even more handsome than you wrote in your book."

Kate laughed out loud. "I didn't want to give away everything, you know. Give the reader a chance to use their imagination."

They spent the rest of the day enjoying the variety of shops—hats, belt buckles, bling, turquoise jewelry, ponchos, and housewares. Kate took Lillie into her favorite shop where a year ago she had found her coveted pair of short cowboy boots. "Oh, these are gorgeous!" she heard Lillie exclaim from behind her.

She turned to see her coveting a beautiful pair of tall black-leather cowboy boots with bright red roses appliquéd on the sides and green vines that wound around the backs to delicately end at the toes. "Those would look fabulous on you, Lillie. Try them on!" Kate encouraged and saw that telling gleam in her sister's eye.

"Well, I guess it wouldn't hurt?" Lillie justified as she quickly found a pair in her size and tried them on.

They fit like a glove.

Kate stood behind her sister, watching her peer into the full-length mirror, turning this way and that to get a better view. She smiled as she remembered how she had felt last year, looking at herself in this same mirror.

"Winner, winner, chicken dinner!" She laughed before adding, "At least that's what Caroline would say."

Lillie turned around grinning. "These are definitely coming with me." She then asked, "How is Caroline?"

While Caroline was Kate's very best friend, she really was part of the family. Years back, when Kate was still in Charleston, Lillie had come to visit and made a stop in Pensacola to stay overnight with Caroline while she performed at the local brewery. While they weren't as close, Caroline was more like an older auntie to Lillie. She was always very generous with gifts over the holidays, particularly after their mother had passed.

"She's as ornery as ever," Kate laughed. "She says hello and hopes that you can catch up now that you are back in the States."

"Oh, I definitely need to reach out to her. Please tell her hello for me!" Lillie said before grabbing the box the boots came in and heading to the register.

Kate picked up her purse and followed. It felt good to be family again. She wondered how that would change once Lillie went away at the end of the week, and she quickly swallowed a lump in her throat. She still had a few more days with her, and she would make the best of them.

They stepped outside, and headed toward Kate's Durango for the drive back to Spicewood. Lillie strutted proudly in her boots. "I could see how you would fall in love with this whole cowboy thing," she said, eyeing her reflection as they passed the storefronts outside.

"There's a reason people fall in love with Fredericksburg." Kate gave her a playful nudge before unlocking the SUV's doors.

As Kate drove, Lillie fell asleep against the passenger-side door. Her dark hair partly covered her sweet face, and she looked peaceful. Kate felt that maternal surge inside her chest as she slowed down to maneuver the curves in the road, trying her best not to wake her. She wondered again about Lillie's plans. When would they see each other again? Taking a deep breath, she looked up while holding the wheel firmly.

I know you have this, and I trust you've got a good plan for us. Then she let out her breath and focused back on the road as they headed home.

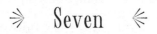

Seven

The next day was bright and clear as they headed out to Port Aransas. Kate sipped on coffee in her travel mug as Lillie watched the landscape unfold before them. The twisting ribbon of road was like second nature to Kate now as she expertly navigated her SUV.

"I packed up some breakfast burritos for the trip; feel free to help yourself," Kate said to Lillie and motioned to the knapsack perched between the seats.

"Ooh, that sounds perfect," Lillie said as she rummaged through the bag and pulled one out.

She took a bite and then hummed, "This is delicious. You know these tortillas are growing on me." She grinned, and Kate laughed back.

"Well, the secret is in the salsa. Verde is my favorite." Kate flicked on her blinker as she pulled up to the light at the junction with 71.

"Remember the sandwiches Mom used to make when we would go driving around the peninsula?" Lillie asked.

Kate nodded. "Yup. The best. Croissant, egg, and Tillamook cheese." She looked sideways at Lillie as she made the turn. "Maybe that's where you began your love for all things French?"

Lillie shrugged as she took another bite. After chewing, she added, "Now I may have to move to Mexico." Part of Lillie longed to go away again somewhere else. Somewhere new. But she knew that soon she would, instead, be headed back to her hometown to face the music.

They drove in companionable silence for a while. The highway opened up, and the mid-week morning traffic was light. Kate turned left onto 281, and they rolled south toward Johnson City.

"You know, it's too bad that we are driving through here during the day," Kate said to her sister. "The Christmas lights in Johnson City are amazing. They go all out, decorating the downtown square and trees all over town in these brilliant blue lights."

"Sounds beautiful," Lillie commented as she wiped her mouth with a paper towel.

Kate had so many things she wanted to talk with Lillie about. So many questions she wanted to ask. Yet, she knew she had to tread lightly. The trip had gone well so far, and she would hate to spoil it with talk of the past.

Instead, she turned on the radio and found a country station.

"Seriously?" Lillie laughed as the singer

lamented his love life and crooned about his old pickup truck and a bottle of beer.

Kate grinned. "When in Rome!"

"How about we ease into this indoctrination?" Lillie said, and she pulled her phone out of her purse.

She plugged it into the Durango's console and then began scrolling until she found what she was looking for. It was quiet for a moment, then Kate could hear this beautiful solo fiddle fill the blank space.

An acoustic guitar picked up with an easy and steady rhythm. She was about to ask who it was when she heard her sister begin to sing in French.

Taking a huge breath, she was glad her eyes were hidden behind her sunglasses. The music was breathtaking, and she realized how much she had missed her sister's unique voice. It was soft and strong as she wove through the melody line, interspersing lyrics with fiddle rides.

When it finally finished, Kate turned to her. "Lillie, that is beautiful. Is that your album?"

Lillie just shrugged as she scrolled to another song. "It was. It's something I was working on with Paul before I left." She queued up another song before adding, "We were planning on putting an album together of just us without the band, but now that's probably not going to happen."

"That's a shame," Kate said to Lillie. "It really is uniquely beautiful. I would buy it."

Lillie shrugged. "Yeah, well, not everything you plan for happens, does it?"

Kate delicately stepped into the opening. "So, what exactly did happen, Lillie?"

Taking a huge breath, Lillie pushed it forcefully out as she looked out the passenger-side window. Finally, she responded, "Oh, it's just a mess." She looked at her sister. "I should have known better than to fall in love with another musician."

Kate kept her eyes on the road and said nothing, hoping Lillie would continue. The song finished, and silence hung between them.

"I guess it all began a year ago," Lillie filled in the quiet.

"We met through a friend when I was looking for a lead guitarist to join the band. Paul came and tried out one night when we played this gig in the Marais, and he fit in perfectly. He knew a lot of our songs already and played the leads tastefully without overpowering the rest of us." Lillie cleared her throat. "However, the thing I didn't account for was how good looking he was. And his voice. Our voices fit so perfectly when we sang harmonies."

Kate could hear the passion in her sister's voice as she continued.

"So, that was it. He went on tour with us for the next year, and we started to get really close. Eventually, we fell in love, which wasn't hard as we were together all the time."

Kate asked, "So, what happened?"

Lillie let her shoulders drop as she looked back out the window to the moving landscape. She fixed her eye on a tower in the distance to slow it down.

"We were on tour in this small town and needed a place to stay the night. Paul said he knew someone. A place where we could crash." She paused. "It seemed like the perfect solution until we arrived. This woman owned the house, and it was clear right away that she wasn't just a friend. She was a former lover of Paul's. Which wouldn't be such a big deal, but you know the French." She stopped, and Kate raised an eyebrow in question.

"Let's just say, I think some French people are a bit looser in their morals. They follow their passions and don't see the big deal with having multiple partners," she finished.

"Oh," Kate said as she waited for more.

"Yeah, it was a horrible evening. We drank

lots of wine, and the whole time they were making eyes at each other, and she kept grabbing for his arm or hand, laughing at all his jokes. He ended up spending the night in her room. I slept on the couch."

"Oh no. What a jerk!" Kate declared, feeling protective of her sister.

Lillie just shrugged again nonchalantly. "It's probably for the best. It would have never worked out anyway. My visa was running out, and he belongs in France."

Kate sighed as she focused on the road. Her instinct was to try to fix it, to figure out a way to make it better. She knew, however, that even when you love someone wholeheartedly, it doesn't always work out. She had found that out with her ex-husband. And now she was afraid Lillie was experiencing the same loss.

Lillie's situation reminded Kate of how messy dating can be. She was grateful to have found Zach—again. Yet, she wondered what issues they would face in the future once the newness wore off. Shaking off those thoughts, she gripped the wheel tighter and took a deep breath.

———

A FEW HOURS LATER they pulled off the highway and drove down a side street until they found the opening to the beach. The sun was bright and the waves playful and beckoning as they drove parallel to the tide line for a while until they found a spot where they could nestle in among the other camper vans and trucks parked on the firmly packed sand.

Kate took a deep breath; she always felt at home near the water. She opened the driver's side door, and the cacophony of birds and kids yelling, along with the smells of campfire, greeted her once again.

"It'll just take a few minutes to get unhitched. If you want to take a walk, feel free!" she said to Lillie as she headed to check the levels on the trailer.

Kate got the coupler off the ball and then pulled her Durango forward before cutting the engine. The sounds of the surf became suddenly prominent, and she watched the outline of her sister as she walked along the tide line looking for shells. Lillie had taken off her sandals and strolled along, allowing her feet to get wet in the Gulf.

Just then, Kate's phone began to vibrate in her pocket. She pulled it out expecting to see Zach's name and instead saw a foreign number. She swiped to answer, "Hello?"

"*Allo?* Is this Kate Summers?" asked a male voice with a heavy French accent on the other end of a seemingly distant line.

"Yes. Yes, it is." Kate answered.

"I am looking for how to get a hold of Lillie? Lillie Summers?" he said in an anxious tone.

"Who is this?" Kate asked him.

"*C'est* Paul. I need desperately to speak with Lillie, but she is not answering her telephone," he said quickly. "Can you get a message to her for me?"

"Yes, of course, Paul." Kate looked out to end of the beach where her sister was walking and tried waving her arm to get her attention, but her back was turned. "She's here with me now at the beach. I can have her call you back?" Kate asked him.

"*Ah, bien.* Please. If you would." He paused, and Kate could hear some noise in the background, like a bar or restaurant.

"Is it true?" he asked suddenly.

"I'm sorry?" she responded, not knowing what he was asking.

"About the baby? Is Lillie with child?"

Kate felt a punch in her gut as she nearly dropped the phone. "Where did you hear this?"

He cleared his throat, and it sounded like he blew out smoke from a cigarette. "A friend of ours here told me, but I could not believe it. Why wouldn't she tell me? Why did she just leave?"

Kate felt distinctly uncomfortable and was anxious to get off the phone and find out directly from Lillie. "I'm not sure, Paul. I'll have her call you back as soon as she can."

They disconnected, and Kate stood staring at her phone screen. Then she looked up to see Lillie turn around and beckon for her to come to the water's edge.

It suddenly all made sense. Her not drinking. The abrupt departure without any concrete plans. The mysterious way she just showed up again after so many years. Lillie was going to have a baby. Kate felt a rush of emotions run through her—worry, excitement, anger. Mostly anger.

She shoved the phone into her pocket, finished securing the trailer, then headed toward Lillie across the shifting sand.

She got to Lillie just as her sister turned toward her with an expression of joy, smiling broadly. "This is exactly what I needed!"

Kate's face was taut as she said, "I just got an interesting phone call, Lillie."

"Oh?" Lillie asked and her smile began to fade as she heard the serious tone in her sister's voice.

"Paul called me." Kate pushed out through gritted teeth.

"Paul? Why would he call you? What did he want?" Lillie asked curiously as the wind whipped her hair across her face.

"He couldn't get through to your number. Seems he wanted to know if a rumor he heard was true." Kate said and then looked at Lillie's belly.

"Is it?" she asked. Lillie instantly knew that her secret was out, and she was relieved and scared at the same time.

"Are you pregnant, Lillie?" Kate spelled it out.

"Yes." Lillie said, and then big tears began to well up in her eyes. "Yes!"

"Why on earth didn't you tell me? What

were you thinking? Were you just going to go back home and never tell me?" Kate asked angrily in rapid fire.

"No! It's not like that. I just didn't know how to deal with it, and I needed to figure out my plan first," Lillie pleaded.

"Why can't you trust me, Lillie? I have been the only one there for you, and for you to do this...".

"There for me?" Lillie's voice began to rise. "There for me? No. You have only been there for yourself." She pointed her finger at her sister's chest as she wiped a tear from her cheek with her other hand.

"You left me to deal with Mom all by myself. Off to Charleston, or touring, or wherever, with David. Your life was so important that you couldn't bother to come home and visit but a few times a year!" Lillie exclaimed to her sister.

Kate's face stung as the accusations flew. "I

did the best I could. You know I had a responsibility in my marriage, to my husband, to be there for him. I couldn't just leave and come home whenever I wanted," she pleaded. "I came back home in the end!"

"When it was too late. When I had already spent months with her in agony and losing her will to live. When I had put aside everything I wanted—my dreams, my hopes, my future—in order to be there for her," Lillie said her voice growing hoarse.

Kate knew she was right, and at the same time she knew she couldn't have done anything differently. She came toward Lillie and put her hand on her shoulder. Lillie shrugged it off angrily and turned away.

The wind whipped up between them and a salty spray slapped their faces. The bird cries echoed off the sand, then were swallowed by the sound of the surf.

"I'm sorry, Lillie. I really am." Kate said, her

voice softer. "I didn't realize how bad it was...I couldn't watch her go." She swallowed hard.

Lillie turned toward her and saw Kate's eyes as full of tears as her own. "It was the hardest thing I've ever done." She sniffed. "Watching her and being able to do nothing about it."

Kate pulled Lillie into her, and they held on as the grief took over. A seagull shrieked above their heads as tears flowed freely down their cheeks. Their bodies shuddered with so many pent-up emotions. They shook and held on tight until there was nothing left to release.

Finally, Kate pulled back as they both wiped their wet cheeks.

"I really am sorry, Lillie."

Lillie nodded. keeping her eyes fixed on the horizon, then finally said, "I know. Me too."

Kate regarded her sister, realizing that the younger woman had far more strength than she had imagined. She had always thought about Lillie as being the weak one, running away.

Now, she knew different. She reached out to brush a wet piece of her sister's dark hair and tuck it behind her ear.

"You are going to be a mother," Kate said gently.

Lillie just nodded and sniffed as a grin broke out across her face.

"And you're going to be an aunt."

Laughter pushed through the pain, and they hugged again before sitting down in the sand to watch the gulf waves caressing the shore.

"Remember when we used to make those driftwood forts at Crescent Beach?" Kate asked as they sat cross-legged in the sand.

"Those were the best," Lillie said. "We would collect all those beautiful, gnarled pieces of wood and build the shelter while Mom dug out the pit for the bonfire."

"Some More S'Mores!" they said together, laughing at the distant memory suddenly so vivid in their minds.

"Mom made the best," Lillie said.

"She was good at a lot of things."

They sat in silence, watching the gentle waves break unevenly, leaving a line of foam and debris as they retreated.

After a while Kate broke the silence. "Are you sure you want to go back to the Northwest for good?"

Lillie dug her toes into the sand, making little arched mounds. "I'm not sure. I do know that I need to get my things out of storage and then figure out a steady job." She kept staring at her feet.

"What about Paul?" Kate asked.

Lillie looked sideways to her sister. "I guess we'll find out."

"What do you want, Lillie?" Kate asked.

Her sister took a deep breath and paused a moment before looking at the horizon. "I want to be with Paul. To have a beautiful baby. To play music, laugh, dance, and sing together as a family."

She then turned to look at Kate, "That sounds like a fairy tale, doesn't it?"

Kate grinned and replied, "Only to someone who hasn't experienced the magic themselves." She hugged her sister. "Fairy tales do come true, and I believe it will happen for you."

They looked into each other's eyes for a moment before letting the landscape of the coast soothe their souls in a way that only time on the beach can do.

Kate knew what they both needed was more faith. They had to believe that it would all work out.

She closed her eyes and said a silent prayer as the wind whipped around and embraced them both.

⇉ Eight ⇇

The next morning, Kate woke early to witness the sun's dramatic entrance. It was silent and magical, as the huge bright golden orb slowly began to lift out of the water right out their bedroom window. The sisters snuggled closer in the bed and just watched as it continued to rise majestically, taking its rightful place above the beach and their tiny silver egg.

"Wow, that was amazing!" Lillie said. "I mean, the sunsets on the West Coast are gorgeous, but getting to see it rise over the Gulf? It was so magical."

Kate took a picture with her iPhone. "That's why I wanted you to come. I didn't even realize the sun rose here like that until I camped out last year. It's now my yearly ritual."

She sent off the picture to Zach with a note: "Good morning! xoxo"

She then squeezed her sister. "OK, I think it's time for coffee, but you're gonna have to move because I can't crawl over you!"

They laughed and tousled with each other like kids before finally both getting up. Lillie sat in the dinette booth while Kate fired up the burner to heat water for their coffee.

Her phone buzzed. "Gorgeous! Headed off to the growers in High Plains. I'll call you later! -XX"

"How's Zach?" Lillie asked.

"Good. He's headed up to the High Plains."

Kate looked up, adding, "They fly on a private jet!"

"Impressive," Lillie said as she watched Kate pour the hot water into the AeroPress before plunging the grounds down.

"Yeah, I forgot what it's like to fly, as I've been driving and living in this camper for so long now. I guess I'll have to get used to it if I plan to go out on another book tour."

"Tell me, how's the sequel coming?" Lillie asked as she hugged the mug of coffee to her chest.

"Well, I got a bit distracted from my fictional life turning into reality these past few weeks," Kate said, laughing. "I'm just getting started plotting it all out, and I'm excited to dig in once you leave." Kate took a sip of her French roast and sighed in deep satisfaction. "Of course, I can't tell you much, but it's going to have some great plot twists."

Lillie smiled at her. "I can't wait. The first one was such a fast read, I am dying to get to the next one."

They sipped their coffee in the dinette while the beach came to life with kids running around chasing fallen kites and dogs playing in the warm water.

"I made Mom's breakfast casserole; it'll just take forty minutes to heat," Kate said to Lillie as she watched her eyes grow wide.

"Oh, that was my favorite! She always made it Christmas Day. I'm so glad you are continuing the tradition."

"I feel like there are some traditions that are old and some new. Like this, for instance." Kate motioned outside the dinette window. "This is new. Waking up to the sunrise. Celebrating the old and bringing in the new year with peace and joy."

She looked at her sister. "Then there's the old ones we love, like this casserole. Even if it doesn't taste the same as when we had it every year as kids, it still brings up those same warm memories."

Eventually, they opened the door to let in the sounds of the beach. Birds calling to each other across the dunes. Dogs running free from their owners in pure delight. One dog was busy digging the deepest hole in the dune. All Kate could see was its stubby white tail sticking up in the air as it dug deeper and deeper, until finally it turned itself around to settle in. Just its white head with two large black patches around its eyes peeked above the sand hole.

After breakfast, they spent the rest of the day lounging around with the waves and alternating between walks to scavenge for shells and resting in the sounds of laughter and the smells of barbecues being fired up.

Toward late afternoon Kate turned to Lillie, "We had better start heading back. With dinner tomorrow night and then your flight out the next morning, that only gives us one more day to explore." She grimaced at the thought of saying goodbye to her sister once more.

"Yeah, depending on how I feel tomorrow, I was thinking it might be fun to just drive around and see more of the hill country," Lillie said.

"Oh, I know. Let's go to Marble Falls for a piece of pie at Blue Bonnet Café," Kate enthused. "It's one of my favorites, and rumor has it that Willie Nelson makes an appearance every now and then."

Lillie's eyebrows raised. "Really? I didn't realize he had a place out here. That is so cool." She hummed a tune to herself as her eyes scanned the horizon.

They packed up their beach chairs and loaded them into the back of the Durango, then Lillie shook out the beach blankets while Kate secured the items inside the trailer.

Before they pulled out, Lillie took her phone out of her purse one more time to take a picture of the beach. She was smiling when she brought it down and then said, "Selfie!" Turning the camera quickly to take a picture of her and Kate together with hair messed up by the beach wind and big salty smiles.

"You better send me a copy of that," Kate declared.

"You bet." Lillie grinned like a kid and winked at Kate.

"Lillie?"

Her sister looked up from her phone with eyebrows raised.

"The beach will always be home," Kate said.

Lillie smiled, "I'm glad we came."

Kate let her gaze rest on a gull high up above them, swooping playfully around until it landed up the beach to scavenge with the other gulls and pipers. The wall of tension between them, the years of hurt and silence healed in an instant.

Gratitude didn't begin to describe the feeling

in Kate's chest as she looked up to the sky:

Thank you.

Nine

When Kate woke up the next morning, it took her a minute to realize that Lillie wasn't beside her. She opened up the windows of her trailer, and instead of the beach, she saw the sunshine beaming at Open Air, her RV neighbors, and familiar sights from her spot nestled in the back of the park.

She was preparing her coffee as her phone rang. She knew only one person who would call her this early: Zach.

"Hello, sleepyhead!" he crooned into her ear as she felt her cheeks blush with warmth.

"Well, hello to you, my vine chaser!" She laughed into the phone. "I want to hear all about your day at the High Plains."

"It was fantastic, Kate." He sounded exuberant. "It was so great to be able to take that private jet and get a chance to ask questions of the William Chris owners. They have been so encouraging and helpful, which honestly surprised me."

"Really? Don't they say everyone in Texas is friendly?" she asked while plunging the press into her coffee.

"Well, they may say that, but wine is a business, and there are so many folks coming in and trying to make a go of it here in the Hill Country," he said. "I think there's also a bit of a rub with folks who want to bring in their wine, or fruit, versus the ones who want to continue making 100 percent Texas wine."

"That makes sense," she said. "I mean, before I went on our tastings last year, I had no idea Texas had so many varietals and made such good wine! Now it's great to see that wine is starting to really gain traction—and I imagine there's a great deal of Texas pride that goes along with that."

"Exactly. Anyone can come up with the money to open a tasting room or winery. Not everyone can make quality wines. I'm learning that it really comes down to two things: growing and selling."

"Tell me more," Kate said as she took a sip of coffee, marveling at how close he felt. She loved how he confided in her as a respected companion.

"Well, growing good, quality fruit is a tough job here in Texas. You remember how they told us at the tasting rooms about the different AVA and terroir?"

Kate murmured her agreement. She

remembered a year ago learning about the American Viticultural Areas— and terroir— that combination of soil, climate, and sunlight unique to certain geographical areas of Texas.

"So, up in the High Plains, which has the largest amount of acreage, they face all sorts of different issues than we do in the Hill Country AVA. We both have issues if there's a freeze, which will kill the vines. But the High Plains has more of a threat of hailstorms. Without the proper netting, which not every vineyard can afford to provide, those grapes will be ruined and never make it to harvest."

"This is all so dramatic and exciting," she encouraged him.

"Right? I am just so thrilled to have found other owners who have the time and wisdom and are able to share what they've learned with me."

He paused for a moment before adding, "You know, Kate, it's not about the money for me. Or even the idea of having my name on a bottle.

It's about the legacy I can leave: one of integrity and pride. I want to make the best damn Texas wines, while also being part of the larger Texas Wine Country community."

"And you will. I have no doubt, Zach. It's one of the things that really attracted me to you: your intention." She longed to feel his breath against her cheek as she sighed silently before saying, "Tell me about the vines themselves. It must have been amazing to see so many."

"Oh, it was magnificent. I got to pick out our blocks from a few different vineyards out there. Mourvèdre. Cabernet. Roussanne. I mean, they look rather puny right now, at this time of year. But these vines have history. Years and years of being top producers in the area. And I'm so excited for our winemaker to do her part after we harvest later this year."

"Her? Wait, I didn't know you had decided on a winemaker." Kate said, a bit confused.

"Yes, Leah. She's one of the candidates

Dennis and I screened, and we are super excited about her expertise. After attending Texas Tech, she interned in California and spent time overseas in Spain, so she knows the Tempranillo grapes well. She, of course, has an affinity toward Texas and wants to make the best Texas wine too," he effused.

"Oh, that's so cool! I mean, there aren't many female winemakers, so that's going to definitely set you apart from the others as well. Good for you!" She laughed. "You know, Dr. Wine, I have to say you are pretty hip."

He laughed a deep belly laugh before saying, "Yeah, right. I'm hip. Wait till I tell Chloe about this."

"Speaking of, she is coming to dinner tonight, right?" Kate asked.

"Yup. She's really excited to meet Lillie. And of course, see you," he said. "But tell me. How was the beach with Lillie?"

"It was like a homecoming," Kate said as

she blew the heat off the top of her coffee and took a sip. "Let's just say that Lillie and I had a long-awaited breakthrough, and it was much needed."

"Ah, good. I'm really glad to hear that. I was wondering how it would be for you both, being together after all the water under the bridge. I'm really glad it went well," he said with warmth lacing his voice.

"Me too," Kate agreed.

"Listen, I'd better get going. We've got our other partner coming in for a meeting after lunch today, and I want to be sure I have everything ready."

"Totally. Zach, I'm so glad that things are going well for you. It's like your dream come true." She paused for a moment before quickly adding, "Mine too."

"Well, we've got a lot more to learn and figure out, but I'm grateful for the guidance from the other, more established wineries. And for your support as well. Kate, you truly make my heart sing."

She blushed. "See you at Otto's at six."

"See you soon!" he replied.

They air-kissed through the phone before hanging up.

She took the last sip of her cup and set it in the sink before turning around in disbelief. How was it that she was actually dating this kind, amazing man?

Sometimes life just works out.

She shook her head in wonder and then began getting things together for a day with Lillie in Marble Falls before they would meet up with Zach for dinner.

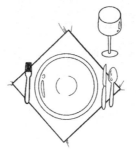

Ten

Kate and Lillie enjoyed a delicious breakfast at the famed Blue Bonnet Café. They sat in a cozy booth and planned out the day's events while nibbling on a generous plate of eggs, hash browns, and a slice of Texas toast.

The place was charming and unassuming. Lillie eyed the case of pies. "I wish I could take one of those with me. That coconut cream looks amazing!"

"I hate to tell you it tastes even better than

it looks," Kate said. "Maybe we can pick up a slice on the way out of town?"

Lillie just groaned and nodded, "Mmhmm," as she took another bite of eggs.

"I can't believe you leave tomorrow. It just seems way too quick," Kate said as she made a face.

"It really did go quickly." Lillie fingered her coffee mug. "I wish you were going back with me."

Kate looked up from her forkful of hash browns at her sister's big brown eyes. She thought about what it would be like to go back there. Back to their old home.

"Maybe I could drive my Airstream up some time to visit?" she said after finishing her bite.

"Oh, for sure! I would love that, sis," Lillie gushed. "Besides, don't you miss the Pacific Northwest just a little bit?"

"Well, I do miss all the gorgeous tall trees and green," Kate remembered. "But I don't miss the rain. However, it might be time to take a break from this cactus terrain and get back to my roots for a bit."

"What about your next book?" Lillie asked her.

"That's exactly what I'm thinking. It might be perfect timing to visit and write some of that scenery into my next novel."

"What about Zach?" Lillie asked as she lifted her water glass.

"I don't think he'd mind. I mean, we're still figuring out our relationship, but he knows I have a duty to my writing and my agent, and he's pretty focused on his winery and getting the tasting room launched." Kate fiddled with a napkin corner. "I think he'll understand and, not only that, be very supportive."

Lillie nodded. "Yeah, he seems like such a grounded, good guy. "

"He does. I just hope it stays that way," Kate said and wiped her mouth with her napkin. She was more cautious after her heart had been broken with David. She had fallen in love with one side of him, only to find out about the other side too late. "It's too soon to be sure, and I'm just trying to take things slow."

Lillie nodded, "You are smart. I always rush in, but see where that's gotten me!" She smirked and rubbed her belly.

"Speaking of, did you talk to Paul?" Kate asked.

"Yes." Lillie said rolling up the corners of her paper napkin. "He wants me to come back to France, but I don't think that's a good idea."

"I would think you'd have more support for the baby here. At least I can come to visit a lot easier here than abroad." Kate said.

"Yes, and I don't have the same health coverage there as I would have here." Lillie unrolled the corners. "I have a lot of research to do yet, and I need to figure out what's best."

Kate looked at her sister and wished she had

answers. Having a baby was a huge responsibility, and she could only imagine how frightening it must be.

"I'm here for you, Lillie." She patted the back of her sister's hand before quickly adding, "I know that you are going to figure this out on your own, but you aren't alone."

Lillie smiled and looked up, "Thanks, sis. I've got a little bit of time to work this out. I just wish that my heart wasn't so confused. I love Paul, but I'm not sure he feels the same. And even if he did, I'm not sure if I can trust him."

"You know what they say: time will tell." Kate said, hating to hear the words herself, but knowing that they were true.

They finished up and Lillie used the restroom while Kate paid the bill. Once outside they waited at the busy intersection before crossing the highway to walk Main Street. The storefronts were still all decked out from the holidays, and Kate delighted in the limestone architecture and small-town feel of it all.

They spent the next few hours wandering about Main Street, poking in and out of shops, looking at housewares, trying on clothes and shoes, and admiring all the unique gifts.

"It seems like everyone here has a hat or boots or both." Lillie grinned.

"There's a lot of ranchers and farmers here. Not sure how many are real cowboys and how many just wish they were." Kate said after a tall man tipped his hat to them as he walked past.

Kate checked her watch. "I think we'd better get back to Fredericksburg."

Lillie nodded and pointed ahead as they made their way up to a red-brick building with three arched windows and a bright-blue painted sign, "Ragtime Oriole." "What's this?" Lillie asked as she peered in through one of the windows.

"Ah, that's one of the oldest buildings on

Main Street, and a great place to grab coffee or wine and enjoy vintage music," Kate said. She remembered ducking in there for a quick cup of coffee last year and delighting in the piano and fiddle music that was playing.

"Maybe they'd be interested in old French tunes?" Lillie mused out loud.

"Ooh, small town Texas is starting to sound good, is it?" Kate teased her.

Lillie grinned shrugging her shoulders. "Maybe?"

Lillie realized in that instant that she wanted to play music again. It had mostly left her after the heartache from Paul and the confusion of her situation. But as she looked through those windows at the piano and music equipment sitting vacant inside, the urge inside her came back. A beckoning of sorts. She smiled at that warm feeling and joined her sister as they crossed Main and headed back to the Blue Bonnet where Kate had parked her Durango.

———

AN HOUR LATER, KATE turned off Main Street and onto Washington, then took a left on Austin Street and slowed down to find a spot. It took two trips around, but she finally snagged a spot across the street from the restaurant as a Ram truck was pulling out.

"We're here!" Kate woke Lillie, who had dozed off during the hour's drive. She let her get situated as she touched up her lip gloss in the rearview mirror.

Kate's phone buzzed.

"Running a little late, but we should have a table already reserved if you want to get settled in."

"Chloe should be there soon too! XX"

She texted Zach back: "No problem. We just got here. See you soon! Xo"

Otto's was tucked away from the busy crowds of Fredericksburg's Main Street. They walked through an enclosed patio to the front doors and made their way to the hostess stand.

"Reservation for Winsome?" Kate asked. Her chest fluttered at the thought of seeing him again. She knew about his partner Dennis and of course had met his daughter, Chloe. The other partner from California she didn't know much about, but she was looking forward to meeting him.

The young man at the stand nodded and said, "Of course. Right this way," and led Kate and Lillie to a back room that had a large table set for six.

Savory smells emanated from the kitchen, and Lillie exclaimed, "Hard to believe, but I'm actually starving again."

They got settled into their seats just as a young woman with dark hair came bustling in.

"Kate!" she exclaimed as she came around to her side of the table. Kate pushed her chair back just in time to embrace her, then turned to introduce her. "Lillie, this is Chloe."

Chloe gave her a hug as well. "I'm a hugger, sorry!" She laughed at herself as Lillie agreed, "Me too!"

They all got settled in their chairs as the waiter came over and filled their glasses with water.

"It is so nice to finally meet you," Chloe said to Lillie.

"How was Marfa?" Kate asked her.

"Fabulous." Chloe said. "I got so much great footage, it's going to take a while to sift through to find the gems."

"I can't wait to see your pictures!" Kate smiled and explained to Lillie, "Chloe is studying digital media arts at UT and is amazing with her camera."

"Ooh! I'd love to see your work," Lillie said.

"And I'd love to hear all about what it was like to be a musician touring abroad," Chloe said.

Kate felt her heart swell as she watched the two girls banter back and forth.

Lillie started to tell Chloe about her experience as a musician abroad, while Kate consulted the wine list and ordered a bottle from the waiter to start. She watched the girls leaning in close and talking feverishly about Paris and thought to herself how perfect this was. After the last few years being alone, here she was sitting next to Lillie. It was well worth the wait, and she wanted to savor each moment. Lillie and Chloe seemed to connect easily, and Kate smiled, thinking about how sometimes everything comes together when you least expect it.

Just then, she saw Zach and two other men come through the main doors, and she waved and smiled over the seated heads. His face beamed, and he bounded up to the table.

"Ladies!" he exclaimed, then hurried to give Chloe a big bear hug and Kate a sweet kiss on her cheek.

"I'm sorry I'm late," he whispered close in Kate's ear.

"You are right on time." She blushed against the heat of his breath on her cheek and squeezed his hand as he pulled away.

"And I see you two have met!" He grinned at Lillie and Chloe, who nodded, smiling.

"I'd like you to meet my partners," Zach said, motioning to the men standing behind him.

"This is Dennis Henke, my dear friend from college," he said as Dennis shook the ladies' hands politely.

"You must be the one that Zach told me about last year with ties to the Newsom family vineyards?" Kate said as she shook his warm hand.

"The very one. But don't believe everything Zach tells you," he said, winking at her and laughing as he squeezed her hand again before turning to shake Lillie's.

"And this is Peter Owens, our financial

advisor and partner who flew in from California," he said as Kate shook his hand as well.

"Pleasure to meet you," Kate said politely.

"The pleasure is all mine. If I'd known how charming this town was, I'd have flown out sooner," Peter said.

They all sat down, and Zach took his seat next to Kate. The waiter came by with the bottle Kate had ordered, and Zach motioned for him to bring another as he poured their wine and prepared for a toast.

"Here's to great partners and what will soon be Winsome Winery in Fredericksburg!" Water and wine glasses clinked, and then they all settled in to peruse the menu.

The waiter brought the second bottle to the table, and Zach filled up Kate's glass before passing it around to the others. "The duck schnitzel is my favorite here, but don't let me persuade you." He grinned at everyone as the waiter came back to take their orders.

Once business was taken care of, they were able to relax into the evening and get to know one another.

"Dennis, tell me about your family. They are German settlers from here, aren't they?" Kate asked as she took another sip of wine.

"Indeed. My great-grandfather settled here in the mid-eighteen hundreds and made a life of farming, corn mostly. It wasn't until recently that we turned some of that land over to vines for growing grapes," he said.

"Wow, I love that rich history," Kate said.

"That history is one of the reasons I'm excited to find the best grapes to make the finest wine for our winery," he continued.

"But you'll also be growing your own grapes too, right?" Kate asked as she looked sideways at Zach.

"Yes, of course. The vines we planted are just matured enough that we may see a good harvest from them in the fall. Depending on that yield, we will likely still supplement with grapes from other vineyards," Dennis explained.

"To get the tasting room doors open, though, we're planning on purchasing wine from other vineyards for this season," Zach said as he topped off Kate's wine glass.

Peter had been listening and chimed in, "That may not be our only source of juice, though," he said, as Dennis raised an eyebrow. "I have some solid connections in Sonoma, and we can always ship that wine out at cost to relabel for the tasting room. It would be a fraction of the cost and the headache of producing and bottling here."

Kate could feel Zach stiffen. "Now, Peter, we've had this discussion, and I think we need to stick with the original plan."

Dennis swirled the dark red wine in his glass as he looked down, his mustache twitching. "We agreed to 100 percent Texas wine, and that's the only wine I'll be making."

In an attempt to lighten the mood, Zach turned quickly to Lillie, "How has your visit been?"

"It's been amazing. I can't believe all the food, the amazing shops, and cute little towns!" Lillie effused. "I definitely wasn't expecting this when I came back to the States, but it's been absolutely charming."

While Kate listened, out of the corner of her eye, she glimpsed Peter typing something into his phone. He was tall and blond, with a smooth complexion that told her he likely had more time inside an office than outdoors in the sun. In contrast, Dennis's face showed deep sun lines etched into his cheeks and barely masked by his large black mustache. He had the face of a rancher.

The waiter arrived with their entrees and made his way around the table to present everyone with their dishes. "Oh, this looks amazing!" Chloe exclaimed as she cut into her schnitzel and then continued to chat with Lillie about her photography studies.

"One of the reasons I knew this winery would work is having Dennis as a partner," Zach said, bringing Kate's attention back to the threesome at their end of the table. "He's got the passion and history in the area, and that's something really important to me. To us," he finished and took a bite of spaetzle.

"And of course, I'm here to make your business a financial success!" Peter interjected as he raised his glass.

Zach paused with his glass midair, "Success comes in all forms. Not just money, Peter."

Dennis cleared his throat.

"Sure. Making the best wine is important, but sometimes just getting the people in the door of the tasting room is the way to start," Peter said. "You can't sell wine if no one is there."

Kate eyed Zach and could see that he was struggling to maintain a neutral face.

"Here's to success on our terms," Zach finally said, and they all took a long sip from their glasses.

Kate's gut hummed as the tension in the room became palpable. It seemed the partners were not entirely aligned on the mission of the winery, and she wondered how they would come to a resolution.

Zach had a way of always seeing the best in things. That was a gift he had. Could it also be a curse? She wondered if he was missing some warning signs.

They finished their dinner with the conversation turning to focus on Lillie's stories from France. Kate looked at her watch and realized that she had better leave soon so that she and Lillie could be ready for the early morning flight out of Austin.

They stood up from the table, and Kate shook Dennis's hand earnestly. "It truly is wonderful to finally meet you, and I'd love to visit the vineyard sometime soon."

"You are welcome anytime, Kate," he said as he brought her in for a bear hug. "Zach is like family, and that means you are now too."

She flushed under his open invitation and thanked him again before turning to shake Peter's hand.

"It was a pleasure to meet you as well, Kate." Peter spoke before she had a chance, and she shook his hand quickly. "You too."

Kate turned away just as quickly and hugged Chloe. "I can't wait to see you again. Maybe I'll come to Austin to visit?"

"That would be great! I could show you around some of my favorite spots," Chloe grinned.

Zach came over to Kate and Lillie. "Come, I'll walk you both out." He smiled warmly at them as he motioned toward the door.

"Be right back!" he exclaimed to Dennis, Peter, and Chloe.

Outside, the chilly air invigorated Kate, and the three of them made their way to her vehicle.

"Lillie, I am so glad I got to spend some time with you, and I hope that you have a safe flight tomorrow," Zach said warmly as he hugged her before she got settled into the passenger seat.

Then he made his way to the driver's side and pressed Kate against the side of the SUV, gently but firmly. "And you," he breathed close. "You." He brushed his hand against her cheek and brought his lips to hers in a deep kiss.

Kate felt a rush go through her body as his lips softly and firmly brushed hers. Pulling away just a little, she felt light-headed from the passion of the moment.

"Gosh, we are really good at that," she laughed to him, and they both smiled and looked into each other's eyes.

"Thank you for coming tonight. I know we

had a lot of business talk, but I'm glad you got to meet my partners," he said as he stroked her cheek with his fingertips.

"About that." Kate hesitated. "Dennis is exactly as I pictured him." She paused and took a breath before adding, "But Peter?"

Zach laughed. "Oh, he'll come around. He's just got to see how we do it here in the Hill Country. He's used to investing in wineries in California with large production. It's different for us, as a boutique winery. He'll adjust." He gave her a squeeze and then one more kiss before pulling away.

"I'd better get back inside." He motioned with his head across the street.

"OK, have a great night, and I'll text you when we get back," Kate said before leaning in to kiss him once more. Then she opened the driver's door and got settled inside.

"Safe drive, Kate," he said and closed the door tightly as she turned on the ignition.

She watched him make his way back across the street and felt happiness in seeing that he was so close to his dream becoming a reality. Maybe Zach was right, and it would all work out. She could just be reading the situation with Peter wrong. If anyone could smooth things out, Zach could. She laughed and shrugged off the unpleasantness. Instead she let her thoughts linger on Zach's sweet, warm, loving kisses. She let those feelings wander through her thoughts the entire long, winding way back.

Eleven

The next morning's drive to Austin Bergstrom airport was quiet. Kate navigated the traffic while Lillie gazed out the passenger-side window, each lost in their own thoughts. Finally, Kate broke the silence.

"Are you sure you'll be OK heading back alone?"

Lillie responded, "Yeah, I'll be fine."

Kate nodded, keeping her eyes on the road. She knew that this was something her sister had to figure out by herself. She just needed to be supportive and trust that Lillie would find her way.

Before long, they arrived at the departures ramp for Alaska Airlines. Kate pulled up to the curb and got out to fetch Lillie's duffel and instruments from the back of the Durango.

They stood on the walkway and gave each other a huge hug. After holding it for a moment longer, Kate reluctantly pulled away.

"You're going to be just fine, Lillie. You'll see. And who knows?" She smiled adding, "Maybe I'll bring my trailer up to visit soon?"

"That would be amazing. We could do beach time...like old times." They laughed and hugged each other again.

Lillie stepped away, put her fiddle case on her back, and then grabbed her guitar with one hand and her duffel with the other.

"Au revoir!" she called out behind her as she made her way to the revolving doors and then disappeared out of sight.

Kate's chest brimmed with sadness, and she brushed away the hot tears threatening to fall down her face.

Godspeed, sweet girl. See you soon.

She got back into her Durango, strapped her seat belt purposefully, then merged into traffic to leave the airport.

Determined not to get all emotional, she thought of the one person who would give her perspective: Margaret.

Her agent was always good at sparking a fire under her butt when she needed it.

At the next stoplight, Kate punched in her agent's contact and waited until she heard the ringing of the phone come over her car's speaker system.

"Well, if it isn't my favorite wine-chasing, best-selling author!" Margaret answered after the second ring.

"Howdy to you too!" Kate laughed and veered to the left to make a turn onto the highway. "I figured I'd check in to see if you had any good news?"

"As a matter of fact, your ears must have been burning, because I was just talking about you!" Margaret's voice grew bright. "We have started planning our marketing and promotion for the next book in the series, and just wait until you see the proofs for the new cover!"

Kate sighed with relief. "Oh, great! I can't wait to see what they came up with. I loved the first one so much, I hope it's similar?"

"Even better. I should be able to get them to you by the end of the day," Margaret said.

"Yay!" Kate felt like applauding.

"Don't celebrate yet. Are you on track with your manuscript?"

"Yes. Yes." Kate chuckled. "I had a little delay with the holidays and my sister visiting, but I should have my final draft to you as promised by my deadline."

"Excellent. We are starting to plan out your

tour and thinking of taking a bit of a different tack on things. Readers are looking for an experience, not just a signing," Margaret continued. "We are looking into some destination tours, weekend meet-the-author events that will bring to life the story and be more appealing to book clubs and larger groups."

Kate nodded as she'd seen what some of her contemporaries had been doing to get their book sales up. With all the competition in the market, it wasn't enough to write a book, even a good one. Thanks to online sales, readers had access to everything at any time. They wanted the personal touch. Something special.

"Well, sure, makes total sense. I'll be interested in seeing what you put together. When do you think you'll have it fleshed out more?" Kate asked.

"Soon," Margaret answered. "I gotta catch this other call, but I'll be back in touch." She hung up before Kate could say anything further.

Margaret was not known for her bedside manner, but she was a damn good agent, and Kate knew that what she lacked in hand holding, she made up for in her dedication to her authors.

Kate thought about how things were changing in the publishing world. Book-tour events were moving away from bookstores and becoming destination events with overnight stays. She was grateful that she didn't have to deal with any of the planning and marketing. All she had to do was write and show up.

Turning onto the ever-familiar Highway 71, Kate looked at the clock: 9:23 a.m. She figured she'd give Caroline a call to see what she was up to. Driving time was always the best time for Kate to catch up on her phone calls.

"Well, hello, my dear! I was just thinking about you," Caroline said brightly when she answered the phone.

"And a howdy to you!" Kate said. "What's happening in the fabulous world of Pensacola?"

"Oh, gawd, you know...the usual. Kids running around like chickens, up to our ears in leftovers, and trying to get everyone to help me take down the Christmas decorations, which is like pulling teeth." She chuckled into the phone. "You sure you don't need to come visit your best friend with some bottles of wine?"

"Oh, you know I'd love to, but I'm on a deadline. I'd better, as my dear agent, Margaret, would say, 'get crackin.'" They both laughed.

"So, how was your visit with Lillie? I've been dying to find out but also didn't want to interfere," Caroline asked.

"It was really great, Car. I mean, we had the best heart-to-heart on the beach, tears and all. We finally talked about the issues with Mom and forgave each other. It was all really amazing."

"Oh, thank the Lord! I've been praying y'all would finally have time together again, just the two of you," Caroline breathed out.

"Well, there's more," Kate said.

"Do tell," Caroline prodded her.

"Lillie's pregnant."

"What?! Oh, my gawd! You're kidding me," Caroline said. "Who's the father?"

"Paul. Her lead or, well, ex-lead guitarist." Kate tried to explain the situation that she didn't even fully understand herself.

"What's she going to do?" Caroline asked.

"She's heading back home to figure it out. She and Paul are talking, too, so that's a good sign," Kate said encouragingly.

"Well, that explains why she came back to the States," Caroline mused.

"She said to tell you she'll call once she gets settled in," Kate told her friend.

"How did it go with Zach and Chloe?" Caroline asked.

"Well, first, Lillie totally adores Zach. And she and Chloe hit it off at the dinner we had at Otto's last night. They are going to keep in touch now that Lillie has gone back to Port Angeles."

"Oh, that's good."

"I just hope that things work out with her and Paul." Kate swallowed hard. "It's so complicated, Car."

"Indeed. I feel for that girl. I mean, I wouldn't want to be in her situation if you paid me. But I know she's a Summers girl, strong and determined. She's going to figure this one out and be the best mama. Just you wait and see." Caroline's voice was soothing to Kate's ears.

"Yes, I'm sure you're right. I'm just glad to be older." Kate considered the seven-year difference in hers and Lillie's ages. "When you are young, it's so hard to say what you feel, and so the communication gets all muddled."

"Oh, yasss. It's not until you get a few rings around the ol' trunk that you start to get the wisdom that comes with perspective." Caroline laughed and Kate joined her.

"You and your southern sayings," Kate said.

"Hey, so how's our Dr. Wine?"

"He's doing really well. I met his partners at dinner, and it's just so exciting to see it all happening," Kate enthused.

"Bravo! I look forward to checking out the tasting room for myself someday," Caroline said.

"Yeah, his friend from college, Dennis, he's pretty awesome. The other partner, Peter, I'm not so sure about," Kate said hesitantly.

"What's Peter's story?"

"Well, he's the partner from California. The money guy," Kate began. "I'm sure he's good at what he does and all, but he made some comments at dinner that got Dennis pretty agitated."

"Like, what?" Caroline asked.

"He seems pretty adamant about bringing California wine here to bottle and sell. I'm still learning about it all, but both Zach and Dennis want to grow and produce 100 percent Texas wine," Kate said.

"Ah, yes. I've seen some articles recently about how Texas wine is making a big splash. It's becoming a major player in the wine industry," Caroline said. "I think Zach's timing is perfect."

"Me too! It's all really exciting to see it happen and to sort of have a behind-the-scenes look into it," Kate said. "I just hope that he can stick to his mission and not have to compromise his ideals."

"Oh, you know those guys from California think they can buy everything," Caroline said. "Peter will learn that in the South, pride is more important than money."

"Indeed," Kate agreed.

Caroline quickly changed the subject, "Let's get to the more important stuff. How's the kissing?"

Kate smiled broadly and said, "It seems like it just gets better and better."

"As it should."

Kate swore she could hear Caroline winking on the other end of the line.

"Well, I've got to giddyup and try and finish

some of these chores before the daylight runs out," Caroline said. "You be sure to keep me posted on everything, right?"

"Of course, I will. Talk to you soon, love!" Kate said brightly.

"Love!" Caroline rang off.

Perfect timing as Kate had just made her way down the winding road and could see the driveway to Open Air up ahead. She took a deep breath and slowed down to the requisite five-mile-an-hour limit, then began thinking about what she wanted to eat for her late break-fast/early lunch. She never got tired of driving through the park, seeing the full-timers and the seasonals as they enjoyed their glamper lifestyles. Kids played in the street, and dogs barked from their tethers as she waved at her neighbors and made her way slowly to her Air-stream. She wasn't sure how long she would live this life, but for now, it was absolutely perfect.

After a bite to eat, she decided to take a walk

around the park to clear her head. As she made her way down the winding road, passing the trailers parked side by side, she let her steps anchor all the emotions swirling around inside. The joy of being reunited with Zach. The past week of conversations, tears, and closeness with her sister. The fears about her sister's future.

It was all too much for Kate to process. In fact, she decided then and there that it was time to dive back into her writing. *The best cure for a messy reality is organized fiction.* She laughed at the absurdity of it, and yet she knew it was true.

Somehow, writing out her characters' lives and stories gave her a sense of control over her own reality.

She rounded the bend and headed direct-ly for her trailer, then pulled her laptop out onto the dinette table. Moments later, she was clacking away on her keyboard, the day's light beginning to turn golden as the sun dropped toward the horizon.

Twelve

It had been weeks since her sister left, and Kate had been making steady progress with her manuscript. Her story was coming to life, and she felt she was beginning to dig deeper into her characters and their motivations. Zach had flown out to California to meet with Peter to talk about their business model and determine how they would move forward with opening the tasting room. He was set to return today and had made plans with Kate to meet for dinner in Austin.

In many ways, Kate was all right with the distance between them. She was still adjusting to having someone in her life after being alone for so long. Although she had prayed for the right man to come into her life, and she was grateful he had, she knew there were compromises she had to make as well. She couldn't just think of her own needs or make plans according to her own wishes. Now she had his schedule, the winery, and Chloe to consider. It was as if her life changed overnight from being single to having a partner. She needed the time and space to adjust to those changes.

Kate was hitting her stride writing and about to finish the next chapter when she saw a text message pop up on her phone.

"Landed. Can't wait to see you! Xo"

Kate just double-clicked the message to "heart" it and then responded, "Me too! See you tonight!" and added a heart emoji.

She turned back to her brightly lit screen,

read over the last paragraph she'd written, and made another edit. Satisfied, she got up from the dinette and poured herself a glass of water. She leaned against the kitchen counter and looked around at the chrome contours of her Airstream.

Turning to the window, Kate watched a truck towing a trailer slowly past her as it made its exit from the park. It was then she caught that whiff of travel. That itch in her to move to another place, to see a different view. She thought about Lillie and their conversation about her taking a trip up there to visit. Maybe now was the time to do it?

She had been struggling with a section of her next book that was set back in the Northwest. For some reason, Kate's writing was geographically influenced. Sure, she could look something up online and describe it as though she had been there. But there was something completely different about being there in person. It's as though the rhythm of the place—the sights, feel, and tastes—transformed her words into something more heartfelt. More real.

While she had been enjoying her time in the Hill Country, becoming more of a "regular" than a tourist, she felt that tug within her to head back to her homeland. Back to the tall evergreens. The misty fog of the coast blanketing the land, leaving a layer of weathered salt in every nook and cranny. The fresh salmon and sturgeon smoked to perfection, only to be paired with a delightful Pinot Noir. It's really where Kate's love of wine was cultivated, and she knew the importance of having food specific to a region paired with wine from that same region.

She thought about Zach's mission of cultivating and sharing the best Texas wine possible. The wines here in the Hill Country spoke to the land they were grown on. It only made sense that to truly enjoy them, one would need to pair the wines with locally sourced food as well. She made a mental note to ask him if his plans included food pairings with the tastings.

Her mind drifted back to the coast and her sister. It was nearing the end of February, and she wondered if the roads would be clear enough for her to make the trip. It was as though her heart decided before her mind, as she instinctively reached for her road atlas behind the dinette bench and opened up to the map of the United States.

The lines of highways crisscrossed the page. The majors ending in "5" ran north to south; I-5 ran up the west side of Washington State from Vancouver to Seattle, then extended up to the border with Canada.

The ones ending in zeros went west to east; I-90 cut across the middle through Snoqualmie Pass and into the heart of Seattle. She traced the smaller Highway 101 from the state capital of Olympia as it arched over the Olympic Peninsula and rested her finger on Port Angeles.

She could almost smell the sea, her memories were that strong.

Looking back out her window at the brown dusty landscape of Texas, she heard the distinctive *chip chip chip*. She caught sight of the familiar flash of red in the branches of a live oak tree. Kate smiled. She knew the cardinal was a good sign that she was on the right path.

Leaving her atlas open on the table, she began humming "Route 66," as she pulled out an outfit for the evening out and laid it on the bed. She couldn't wait to tell Zach her plans. Her pulse sped up when she thought of the adventure she'd have driving with her new trailer across the western part of the country. *Home is where you park it.* She laughed and then got ready to jump into the shower.

⇒ Thirteen ⇐

Kate slowed down on Highway 71 and waited for the steady stream of traffic to pass before she turned left into the parking lot at Jack Allen's Kitchen. Founded by Jack Allen Gilmore, this local chain focused on cultivating a relationship with the ranchers, growers, brewers, and producers in the area. It was literally farm to table, as they created a seasonal menu around the local bounty and shared it with patrons in a relaxed, no-nonsense atmosphere.

Kate pulled into a spot and cut the engine.

She glanced quickly in her rearview mirror to check her lip gloss and tussle her blond hair before heading inside the restaurant.

Once inside the glass front doors, she was greeted by the gentle cacophony of conversation, silverware clinking against plates, and sizzling sounds from the kitchen. She made her way up to the hostess stand and then saw Zach wave at her from across the open room.

Kate's heart skipped a beat as she broadly smiled, waving back, and made her way over to meet him. Zach stood up and waited for her to navigate her way to him before enveloping her in a big bear hug. They held on for a while, and Kate luxuriated in the feeling of his big strong arms around her. She tilted her head up and their lips met, lingering for just a moment before they pulled away. Zach held her chair out for her as she got settled and then returned to his seat and placed a napkin back over his lap.

"It's so good to see you," he said.

She blushed and unrolled her napkin. "You look even better than when you left, if that's possible."

"Well, I'm sure glad to be back. California is sunny and beautiful in its own way, but there's nothing like the great state of Texas," he said and picked up his menu.

"I can't wait to hear all about your trip. I've been wondering how things went, and I've got some news of my own!" She winked.

"Really?" His eyebrow cocked as he looked over his menu.

"Yes, but we have plenty of time. Let's order first."

"Perfect. I'm famished from the long day of travel."

They considered their menus, and both agreed to the signature house margarita on the rocks. Kate decided on the grilled ruby trout with sun-dried tomato walnut pesto and apple-pecan relish, while Zach chose the chorizo-stuffed pork tenderloin medallions in roasted-garlic cream sauce.

After the waiter took their order, they settled back to enjoy the ambiance and each other's company. Kate marveled at how intimate it was to share a meal with someone. Maybe it was the last few years of eating alone, but she was acutely aware now of how special it was.

"So, tell me about your trip," she said.

He adjusted in his seat before responding. "Well, it was good for the most part. I mean, Peter took me around to some of the major wine producers in Sonoma and Napa, and I got a chance to ask questions and get advice."

"I imagine it's probably much different to produce wine in California than in Texas? I mean, just the history alone must be intimidating?" she asked.

"In some ways, yes. I mean, we also have our own history here in Texas of growing grapes and making wine, but it's definitely not at the same scale or length of time. Surprisingly, we are catching up quickly, though. I believe Texas is now one of the fifth largest wine-producing states in the US, which is sort of amazing, really, if you think about it."

He paused as the waiter delivered their cold salt-rimmed glasses of margarita. They each took a sip and hummed in delighted agreement before Zach continued.

"Where we are different is the terroir and the scale of production," he said. "The producers Peter took me to boasted about their state-of-the-art facilities and the consistency of their large batches." He paused to take a sip.

"But that's not what you are building here. A boutique, small-yield winery has to be vastly different, right?" she asked.

"Exactly. It's peaches to oranges, if you'll excuse the bad idiom. And frankly, I don't expect we will ever be that large. At least that's not the vision I have for the winery."

Kate said, "You always said you wanted to keep it small and manageable."

"Precisely. I just don't think Peter understands this. He sees our wine production through California-tinted glasses. Unless we can come to a better understanding soon, we may have a real problem." Zach fingered the condensation on the sides of his glass.

"I'm sure you'll be able to figure it out, but I really hope you don't compromise your goals." Kate said. "It's just like this place"—she nodded to the room—"they are dedicated to doing this all with locally sourced vendors. I'm sure it would be much cheaper to just ship in bulk from Sysco or some other supplier, but that would make it just about the bottom line. And we'd miss out on tasting authentic regional cuisine."

"Not only that," he added, "by supporting local, they are helping to build a sustainable food source that feeds generations of families. Wine is just like that: it's ranching."

He looked at her with his blue eyes shining brightly. "I want to ensure that we are taking care of our land and that our vines will sustain for generations."

"Speaking of locally sourced," Kate ventured, "I was thinking the other day about some of my favorite food and wine from the Northwest and how when they are sourced from the same place, they can bring out the best in each other. Are you planning on doing any food and wine pairings at the winery?"

Zach nodded vigorously, "Absolutely. We'll just have to be a bit creative at first. We aren't set up to be a restaurant with a full menu, but I would like to approach some of the local chefs to see about doing pop-ups or special tasting events."

"That sounds amazing," Kate said just as their food arrived and the plates were placed in front of them. "And this looks amazing!"

They each dove into their dishes and let

their taste buds overwhelm their senses as they enjoyed those first hot bites.

Zach wiped his mouth with the corner of his napkin. "Enough about the winery, tell me about you. How's your writing coming? How's Lillie?" He smiled gently at her, and her heart warmed to his words and the food that was settling in her belly.

"The book is coming along, although I've had a bit of a rough patch trying to work through some timeline issues." She took another swallow of her margarita. "Lillie's doing well but still trying to sort some things out. Her pregnancy is going smoothly so far, thankfully." She paused for a moment, wondering if now was the best time to tell him her plans.

"That's good to hear. You know, maybe you should take that trailer of yours out there and visit her before the baby comes?" he said as he pushed his food around on his plate, trying to get a forkful.

"It's like you're reading my mind," Kate said, thinking about how uncanny it really was. "I think that is exactly what I'm going to do."

Zach raised his head with his eyes wide open. "Really? When do you think you'll go?"

"Well, I think soon. I'd like to go up there and come back before your winery opens, and honestly, I think it will help me to get past this hurdle I'm having in my book. It's based in the Pacific Northwest, and I think being back there will help me describe the setting better."

Zach just grinned at her and said, "That makes perfect sense."

Kate felt immediately relieved. In her marriage, she had felt frustrated not being able to make the decisions she needed to make without meeting resistance. Many times, she had wanted to come back home to the Northwest yet was unable to by herself. David insisted that they be together all the time, but with his busy schedule, it was impossible to find the time away. She swallowed down the bitterness of that regret, wondering what would have been different if she had been able to visit more before her mother passed away.

Now, she was determined to make better choices, and not let someone else dictate for her. She watched Zach as he methodically cut his tenderloins. Here was a man who was secure enough with himself that he wasn't afraid to let her travel where she needed to alone. It wasn't as though he didn't care. In fact, she knew he cared a great deal. But he trusted her.

And, perhaps, he trusted himself as well.

"You know," Zach said, placing his napkin beside the plate. "I've been thinking about our own situation here. I know it's difficult with me sharing a space in Austin with Chloe, and we hardly have any time to be together with my traveling back and forth to the winery." He trailed off for a moment, then reached over the table to Kate.

She placed her hand in his and immediately felt tingles of electricity run up her arm.

"I was thinking that maybe I'd get a place closer to the winery. Maybe in Fredericksburg, Stonewall, or Comfort." He said as he squeezed her hand. "Maybe a place you could come stay?"

Kate's eyes opened wide as she tried to swallow. "Um, well..." she stammered as her heart began to beat wildly in her chest and she resisted the urge to pull her hand away from his.

"I know it's soon, but I would love to be able to spend more time together," he said in a rush. "I think Chloe is set up now, and she even has a friend interested in moving in." He stroked her hand delicately. "And I would love the opportunity to wake up next to you." he concluded softly.

Kate felt the strong pull of their attraction. At the same time, she felt a flight response building inside her. "What about my Airstream?" she asked as she found her voice again.

"Well, it could just be a part-time situation? Or maybe we could find a place you could store it nearby?"

Kate's hand went cold and rigid. "No. I'm not ready for that," she blurted out and pulled her hand back.

Zach's face looked crushed for a moment before he regained his composure. "Of course. I mean, I know we're still getting to know each other," he tried to reassure her.

Kate's heart beat rapidly. She took a deep breath and then looked up into his beautiful eyes. "I mean, I know that's what I want eventually." She took another deep breath. "I just didn't think that would happen so soon." She fingered the edge of her napkin, struggling with her conflicting feelings. She wanted desperately to be with him and, at the same time, was terrified of losing herself again.

The waiter came to deliver their check, and Zach took care of the bill while Kate excused herself to use the restroom. She stared at her reflection in the tall mirror and shook her head as tears threatened to come. What was she thinking? That a man would be all right with her living in her own trailer and want to live apart indefinitely? She felt foolish and disappointed. She loved her Airstream and was just getting comfortable in her new life. Would she have to give that up in order to be in this relationship? Why was she always the one to make the compromises?

She thought back to how it was always on David's turf before. It was his house, his friends, his life, his everything. And once she chose to stand up for herself, her nothing. She couldn't go through that again. She couldn't risk her heart again like that.

She blinked her eyes, coming back to the present and realizing that it might be an impossible situation.

She exited the restroom and met Zach at the

entrance as he put his arm around her waist. They walked back to her Durango in silence, just the whoosh of cars speeding by to break through the moment.

Once they reached the driver's side, Zach gently turned her toward him. "Kate."

She looked up at him, her eyes glistening despite her desire to not cry.

"Kate, I have no intention of rushing into anything. I want you to feel comfortable."

She nodded, sniffing slightly as he lifted her chin up delicately and placed his sweet lips over hers. Softly, gently, they kissed. His tongue beckoning hers, as they leaned closer together, and she pressed against his chest, her fingers caressing the nape of his neck. The electricity washed away her nerves as they pulled each other closer, their desire taking over. Her entire body felt alive, and she longed for nothing more than to stay this way forever.

When they finally pulled apart, she dropped

her hand to his chest, feeling his heart beating beneath her palm. Zach ran his thumb softly against her cheek.

"There's no rush," he said, catching his breath.

Kate wanted desperately to say something, to try to explain, but she knew that she needn't. He understood her in a way that she was still trying to figure out for herself. She just wondered how long he would wait, and that gave her a chill deep inside, knowing that she would have to make a decision at some point in the near future.

They kissed again and said their goodbyes before finally getting into their vehicles. Kate pulled out going west toward Spicewood; Zach turned east, back to Austin.

⇛ Fourteen ⇚

The next morning, Kate woke feeling groggy. She had spent the night struggling to find sleep, while her mind flip-flopped the situation unrelentingly until dawn. Kate knew that she was partly reacting out of fear from her past experience. She also knew that she presently loved her new life and wasn't ready to give that up yet.

She got up to make herself coffee and looked at her atlas open on the dinette table. If there was anything Kate knew, it was that she did her best thinking on the road. Something about those mile markers ticking by gave her a sense of purpose and control. The power of firmly holding the steering wheel in both hands and driving toward the horizon, not worrying about the destination, just being in that moment. She always felt like it was a safe cocoon where she could let her mind wander as her eyes took in the changing scenery.

Now was the perfect time for her to go. She needed to think about her new relationship and have the space and time to do that. She also needed to find the missing piece that would truly make her manuscript sing. Kate felt the maternal tug toward Lillie, as her baby sister was getting closer to her due date. After their time on the beach, she felt close to her sister again, and she was determined not to let that change. Now that she had a home with wheels, she had no reason not to visit her. Kate marveled again at how the pieces of life come together in the most unexpected ways.

She poured half-and-half into her mug and then cozied up in the dinette to begin planning her trip. She would take the most direct route up, traversing the west side of the Rocky Mountains, crossing through Utah to Salt Lake City, then skirting the lower left-hand corner of Idaho and crossing into Oregon. Instead of taking I-90, she'd avoid the mountain pass and follow the southern route along the Columbia River. At Portland, she'd turn north on I-5 toward Olympia where she would veer off to head toward the Peninsula.

Kate knew it was still a bit early in the season, and she was careful to plan a route that avoided mountain passes or long stretches on smaller highways. As long as she stuck to the majors, she would be all right, as those roads had enough truck and regular traffic to keep the threat of ice at bay. Kate decided to do the trip as quickly as possible, 2200 miles in six days. It was ambitious, but she wanted to have as much time as possible with Lillie before needing to head back.

A shiver of excitement ran through her as she planned her waypoints and calculated her mileage. Her first cross-country trip with the trailer! She loved to drive long trips but figured she'd better factor in slower speeds and more fuel stops towing the trailer. She settled on the average day's trip being around seven hours, or four hundred miles. The final two stops once she got into Washington State would be shorter and likely a welcome break from road fatigue.

First stop: Carlsbad, New Mexico. She'd found a winery where she could boondock overnight. One of the perks of being a Harvest Hosts member, she could stay for free on the property as long as she purchased a bottle of wine. Second: Durango, Colorado. It was a long stretch, but she remembered how she loved that town on previous travels with her ex-husband and wanted to stay there again, even if it was just overnight. Third night: north of Salt Lake City, where she'd found a KOA that looked decent and safe. Fourth: La Grande, Oregon. Just on the other side of the border, she found a resort that boasted of mineral hot springs. She figured she'd definitely need that after the long day's drive. The fifth night would land her in Washington State, and she'd stop at Silver Lake, midway between Portland and Olympia and with a view of Mount St. Helens. Finally, after six days of travel, she'd end up in Port Angeles, Washington.

Kate made the reservations and then leaned back into the dinette cushion, looking around her tiny home. She couldn't wait to leave. It had been years since she had done a long road trip like this, and the timing couldn't be more perfect.

She dialed Lillie and proceeded to share her plans. "Sis! I can't wait to see you. You won't believe how much has changed here, and I have so much to tell you!" Lillie effused as Kate explained her itinerary.

"I'll see you in six days, God willing!" Kate said.

"That's a lot of driving time. Be safe, and call me if you need to talk."

"I will. I have a lot to think about, and I'm hoping the road will help me to work through some of my ideas for the manuscript," Kate said.

"Sounds good, sis." Lillie said, then added, "Enjoy the journey!"

Kate smiled to herself as she thought about how Lillie had called her brave on the beach. She didn't feel very brave most of the time, and she had to admit she was intimidated by towing a trailer for such a long trip. Yet, she felt reassured by the thought of so many solo travelers, women she'd met online through the

Girl Camper group, who did this every year. It gave her the courage to believe she would be fine. It was just like anything new—at first it seems daunting, and soon it becomes second nature. Kate was hopeful that this trip would not only provide her with a clear headspace and focus for her writing but also give her even more confidence by showing her just what she could handle on her own.

As she got settled for the night, she watched the sun set a brilliant burnt orange on the horizon and the wisps of feathered clouds moved across the sky, reflecting yellow and pink against the deepening blue of the night. She wondered what the sunsets would be like on her journey and said a silent prayer of protection for herself and her new home.

⇒ Fifteen ⇐

It was a brisk, sunny day as Kate traveled through Utah, gradually gaining elevation. The first night in Carlsbad had been so windy that she'd grabbed a bottle of wine from Balzano Vineyards before retreating to eat dinner inside her trailer. Those four hundred miles had been mostly uneventful as she drove through the dusty landscape of West Texas, before making her way into New Mexico. She'd passed oil fields and seemingly endless barbed-wire fences just off the highway stretching as far as she could see. Remnants of plastic bags caught up in the barbs flapped wildly in the gusts of wind as she drove past. Flags of futile desperation.

The second day found her cutting through New Mexico and across Albuquerque, passing by the Navajo Nation as she drove across the desert terrain. Just before nightfall, she reached Durango to stop for the night. It was cold, but Kate sat outside for a moment, taking in the stars. She wondered if they seemed closer due to the elevation. She felt comforted by their number and slept that night with the windows open, welcoming the sharp clean air as she fell fast asleep. By morning, the temperature in her trailer had dropped to thirty-six degrees, and Kate quickly turned on the furnace to heat things up as she prepared her coffee for the drive.

The third day's drive grew more eventful as she made her way west from Colorado and into Utah. The terrain became more jagged and rocky, and before she knew it, she had reached

Moab. Beautiful red rock formations seemed to appear out of nowhere and majestically hugged the highway as she wound her way on the edge of Arches National Park. Kate longed to stop and see the natural monuments for herself, but she didn't have the time to spare. Another trip she would come and visit. Maybe with Zach?

For much of the drive, he was not far from her thoughts. She felt as though she had pressed the pause button on her life back in the Hill Country—and the reality that she would need to make decisions about her new relationship, something she wasn't yet sure about herself. She needed more time.

Her thoughts would flit past with the scenery. She'd settle on one, letting it turn over in her mind, and then it would be gone again with another taking its place. Lillie. Her mother. Zach. Caroline. She watched a hawk spiraling ahead in the clear sky. Just the rhythm of the road kept her tethered. She looked through her rearview mirror at the silver egg solidly attached to her Durango. Kate smiled, thinking that she was actually doing it: towing her own trailer across the country.

She then thought of her ancestors. She always felt closer to them when she drove in long stretches of desolate land. How did they manage this landscape by horse and wagon? She remembered reading journal entries from the trip across the Oregon Trail and shuddered at the thought. The uncertainty, rough terrain, disease, and danger. It was in these moments that Kate felt that her own accomplishment of towing a trailer paled in comparison. They had the true courage and guts.

On and on her thoughts fluttered by, without resolution. Just a comforting blanket of memories, real and imagined. Kate pressed her foot on the accelerator as she sped forward toward Salt Lake City where she would spend the night.

Four days into the trip, and her destination

for that evening was La Grande, Oregon. The long days of travel were catching up with her. Kate's mind turned to negative thoughts as she grew more physically weary. She resorted to energy drinks to keep herself alert, but felt the general weariness settle into her bones. Twenty-six-mile-per-hour wind gusts through Idaho on I-84 pounded her trailer, forcing her to slow down, which made the day's travel even longer. As she wound her way along the Snake River, the gusts grew stronger, and Kate wondered if they would ever let up.

She passed the town of Ontario with a half tank of gas, planning to stop at the next station before she hit Baker City. After barreling along for some time, she looked down at her gas gauge and saw she had thirty-five miles left in range, with no gas stations in sight. She looked on her GPS for the closest station, and it was in Baker City—thirty-one miles away.

Kate gulped down her panic. Fear brought

her fully awake with the dread that she may end up stranded in the middle of nowhere. She downgraded her speed to not use up any excess fuel, silently cursing herself that she hadn't just stopped to fill up in Ontario.

With fifteen miles left, she hit the top of the hill that sloped down toward Baker City. She slowed to forty-five miles per hour, put her hazards on, and let her foot off the accelerator, coasting down the hill. Her gas gauge finally dropped to LOW, and she had no idea if she would run out or not. She said a prayer as she pulled off at the next exit and coasted, leaning her body forward as if that would help her get to the station quicker.

Five long minutes later, she slowed through the small town and saw the Chevron station ahead. Still holding her breath, she pulled up to the pump and cut her engine, her heart beating wildly.

She filled the tank up and realized upon

calculation that she had less than a gallon of fuel left.

Thank you.

La Grande was just thirty minutes ahead, and Kate was relieved to finally pull in for the night. She had made it to Oregon and was more than halfway done with her trip. As she set up camp, she made sure to connect an electric water hose as it was going to drop below freezing overnight.

Then she made her way to the hot springs pool behind the office to soak before crawling into bed and passing out.

The next morning, she called Zach as she met up with the Columbia River and followed it west toward the Dalles and Portland.

"Kate! That's scary!" Zach said as she recounted the previous day's events and nearly running out of gas.

"I suppose I would have been OK if I had run out, but who knows how long it would have taken for someone to come out from AAA?" she said as she sped along I-84.

"I know I'm not supposed to say this, and I'm sure you would have been fine, but that scares the hell out of me, thinking of you alone in the middle of nowhere like that." Zach said with fear lacing his voice.

Kate breathed in and let it out in a long sigh. She appreciated his concern, which echoed her own, "Don't take this the wrong way, but it was one of the times on this trip I really wished you had been with me," Kate reflected. "I love to travel alone to be with my own thoughts, but it's times like that when I realize just how lonely and frightening it can be."

"I'm really glad you made it OK." Zach's words felt like a warm hug over the phone.

"Enough about me and my excursions. What's happening with you and the winery?" Kate thankfully changed the subject.

"Well, I'm afraid I haven't made much more

progress than when you left," he breathed into the phone. "I've been on conference calls with Peter all week, and he's getting more vocal about wanting to open the tasting room on his terms."

"And what are those terms?" Kate asked as she carefully maneuvered the narrowing highway past Hood River.

"He wants to see his investment pay off sooner and feels that we can make better wine in California and then ship it out for less cost," Zach said, exasperated.

"Didn't he like the Texas wine he tried during his trip?" Kate asked.

"It's not that he didn't like it. He agrees that Texas wine is just as good as California wine on a taste basis. But he's more concerned with the cost and scale, and I think he's also made some deals with producers in California as part of his investment."

"Really? Did you know about that before?"

Kate shook her head to herself as she thought about how life never turns out how you expect.

"No. I didn't. And that's why I'm pretty upset about this." Zach cleared his throat. "I just don't know what I can do at this point. If I stick with the mission of 100 percent Texas wine, I will likely lose him as an investor." He exhaled loudly. "I just don't think I can afford to open if that happens."

"Oh, Zach. I'm so sorry. There has to be a way to work this out," Kate said, trying to reassure him. "Maybe you could find another investor?"

"That's what I'm working on now. I've been talking with my former partners from back East and may be able to get them to come in as more silent partners."

"That may be the best thing. If someone doesn't know about making wine in Texas, or have a passion for it, they may just focus on the numbers as well and miss the heart of it."

"Precisely."

"I'll be praying that something comes through for you," Kate said with conviction.

"Something will. It always does," Zach responded. "Be safe out there, and I'll be waiting for your text tonight."

"I'll finally be back in Washington!" Kate said excitedly as the realization hit her that she'd be seeing Lillie in a day.

They rang off, and Kate spent the next part of her drive wondering about the business of wine making and whether Zach would figure out a solution. She had that instinct to try and help but didn't know how. She certainly didn't have money to invest, and she didn't know enough about the industry to be more helpful. She finally settled on the fact that she would do more research and just try and be encouraging. It was Zach's dream, and she knew he wouldn't let it go without a fight.

She thought about how even keeled he was.

Kate wasn't sure she would have had the same response. Likely, she'd be cursing Peter but would definitely be more upset. Yet, that was another quality of Zach's she liked: He wasn't afraid to say how he felt, but he didn't dwell on those feelings. He was kind and methodical about finding a solution. She smiled to herself at his determination, and her mind traveled to the memory of his warm lips on hers. She grinned and felt that familiar rush of dopamine, letting those thoughts linger for a while longer as she drove on toward Silver Lake.

⇾ Sixteen ⇽

Kate awoke with anticipation tingling through her as she realized she was just a few hours away from the Olympic Peninsula. What seemed to be such a long distance out was that much closer. She grinned and texted Lillie: **Made it to Washington! PA today!**

Bubbles formed and Lillie replied, **Can't wait!** with a heart-face emoji.

Kate was delighted at the thought of being so close to her sister. She picked up her coffee and stepped outside her trailer to breath in the cold, damp air. It was a rare sunny morning, and light refracted off the dew, making the evergreens sparkle with the new day. Mount St. Helens appeared in the distance, and Kate saw its reflection in the flat lake. She was majestic even with her top blown off. Kate grinned as she felt the familiar tugs of home. All the dust and dirt and miles, and here was her reward.

Taking a sip of coffee, she shivered slightly from both the cold and the anticipation of today's travel home—just three hours away. She felt like a school kid and hurried back to her rig to prepare to head out.

The traffic on I-5 heading up toward Olympia was thick and steady, and Kate breathed a sigh of relief once she merged onto Highway 101. The tall thick trees lined the sides of the highway, concealing the view beyond, but Kate could almost smell the water. The closer she got, the more she felt as though she were being guided. She reached Discovery Bay and then followed the highway along the peninsula with the Strait of Juan de Fuca teasing her along the way.

It had been a few years since she had driven these roads, but nothing had changed. She still saw the same boats in dry dock sitting up along the highway and the same roadside stands where locals sold flowers and honey. She passed through the downtown streets where the water opened up beyond. The highway took her past the pier where the ferry shuttled passengers across to Canada. She could see the outline of land appearing like a floating mirage.

Kate continued farther and then turned off the highway onto smaller roads until she saw the familiar signs for Salt Creek. She passed by, and the road narrowed until it ended at her destination: Crescent Beach RV Park.

She stepped out of her rig at the office and peered across the road at the sand dunes. Her heart tugged as she took in the familiar sights of driftwood, sand, windsocks flying, and surf pounding. It was just a month ago that she and Lillie were talking about this while on the beach at Port Aransas, Texas. Now, here she was seeing it in real life. It was all incredibly surreal.

Kate checked in and then found her spot up the way and nestled her rig against a thick backdrop of pine trees. She hurried to get set up, hearing the sounds of the beach beckoning her. She crossed the private road and walked up through the dunes and sawgrass, then maneuvered around a thicket as the beach opened up before her.

Ocean waves pounded the shore, and Kate watched as surfers took their turns trying to tame the wild waves and ride in one after another. She took a deep breath, the salt air washing away every part of the long journey. She took out her phone and snapped a picture, then sent it without a word to Lillie.

She heard the ding on her phone as Lillie

"hearted" the picture. Bubbles, then, "Welcome back!"

⇒ Seventeen ⇐

After a good night's sleep, Kate headed back toward Port Angeles. She took Marine Drive to where it veered to the right on First Street, then headed a few blocks up to where she would meet Lillie, at the Next Door Gastropub. Her mouth watered as she craved sinking her teeth into the "Not Your Average Joe" burger: coffee-rubbed beef topped with bacon, pepper jack, ale-battered onion straws, and tangy aioli. It was heaven on a toasted bun.

Kate found a spot to park her Durango on the street half a block up, then walked back down the main street of town, reveling in the familiarity of the place. She craned her neck to catch a glimpse of her sister.

Lillie had texted her fifteen minutes earlier that she had already arrived and was waiting for a table. One of the busiest eateries in town, the Gastropub did not take reservations, and there was generally a line of customers waiting outside.

Just then, she spied a flash of arm waving and saw Lillie smiling at her. She picked up her pace, and they met out front in a big bear hug.

"You made it!" Lillie squealed in delight as she hugged her sister.

"I almost don't believe it!" Kate said as she pulled away to get a better look at Lillie. She was just beginning to show, and there was a glow about her lovely face.

"I put our name on the list, and Meg's

working, so we should be able to squeeze in here pretty quickly," Lillie said.

"How is Meg?" Kate asked, remembering her sister's friend from high school.

"She's doing awesome. I'm really grateful that I've been able to stay with her and Rick. They have been lifesavers while I figure out my next steps," Lillie gushed as they stepped back to let an elderly couple pass on the sidewalk.

"I'm so glad that worked out. Has it been good to catch up with everyone?" Kate asked, shielding her eyes from the midday sunlight.

"Yeah, it's funny. I thought it would be super weird coming back after being away so long, but everyone has been really welcoming. Some things have changed, but mostly it's like I never left."

Just then, the hostess waved to Lillie, and they made their way inside to their small table against the wall.

A woman with short blond spiked hair came

up to their table. "Kate! It's great to see you," Meg said as she hugged Kate and then gave Lillie a squeeze. "Can you believe our songbird decided to come back home?"

Lillie laughed and swatted her playfully.

"I, for one, am glad she's back," Meg said and then turned to Kate. "And, what about you Miss *New York Times* Best-Selling author? How long will you be here for?"

"Not long enough," Kate grinned. "I just wanted to check on Lillie, and I'm hoping to finish my next novel here before I leave."

"Excellent. You are welcome here anytime," Meg winked. She then turned as someone called her name and excused herself to check on another table.

"I can't believe she's running this place now." Kate said. She remembered Meg as the young girl Lillie used to pal around with in junior high, then high school.

"Yup. She and Rick have been at it for two

years now, and it seems to really suit them both. Everyone here raves about them as a team." Lillie set the menus aside. "We don't need these, right?"

Kate shook her head, "You know what I want."

Lillie grinned. "Me too."

The place was packed for lunch, and they chatted for a bit as Kate told her about her travel adventures, and Lillie filled her in on happenings around town.

"I got a gig at Bourbon West once a month. And there's some other places in town that are going to get back to me," she enthused. "It's not steady yet, but at least it's a start."

"I still can't believe what happened at Castaways," Kate said incredulously. She had heard news that the longtime waterfront restaurant and lounge had burned down to the pier a month before.

"Right? Our local hangout. It's such a shame. They are still investigating, but it doesn't much matter now that it's gone," Lillie said as she placed a napkin over her lap.

"Have you thought about teaching?" Kate asked.

"Yeah, I may do some private lessons." Lillie grimaced slightly. "It's not my favorite thing, but it could be a good source of steady income."

The burgers came, and they both let out a moan and dug in. Kate couldn't believe it tasted just as good as she remembered. Maybe some of the best things don't change?

They were both quiet for a bit, enjoying each bite, until finally Kate wiped her mouth and asked, "How's the baby?"

Lillie got the cutest expression on her face as she murmured through a mouthful, "She's growing bigger each day. I had my second-trimester ultrasound!" She dug into her bag and pulled out the black and white rectangle for Kate to see.

Kate wiped her hands well and then held

the edges of the picture. She could just barely make out the baby's sweet face as though she were happily floating along.

She looked back at Lillie with big eyes. "Wow! I can't believe how much you can see so early?"

Lillie nodded, "Yeah, it's amazing how quickly she's developing. Kind of scary, really." She fingered the picture gently before placing it in her bag. "I hope I'm ready."

Kate looked at her sister. "Well, it won't much matter because she's gonna come either way."

They both laughed.

"Have you talked with Paul?" Kate ventured.

"Oh! Yes." Lillie finished another bite of food as Kate waited anxiously for the response.

"He's coming to the US!" Lillie beamed.

"Really?"

"Yeah, we've been doing a lot of talking over the past month, and I realize now that perhaps I was a little hasty in judging the situation."

Lillie shrugged. "He says he wants to be with only me and is willing to move here to prove it. I owe it to him to give it a shot."

"Wow. I think that's really good news, don't you?"

Lillie nodded, "Yes. I mean, I do miss him, and I really want it to work out."

Kate smiled. "I bet it will. I can't imagine anyone not wanting to be with you, Lillie. You are a very special woman."

Lillie blushed. "Takes one to know one."

They finished their lunch, waved goodbye to Meg, and then headed out onto the sidewalk.

"I've got to get back to my manuscript, but how about we get together this weekend?" Kate asked.

"Hey! I have a gig next week at Bourbon West. You should come and then we'll grab a bite after!"

"Perfect. I can't wait." Kate smiled broadly and encircled her sister in a hug.

"See you later, gator."

"After a while, crocodile."

They went their separate ways and Kate felt better about Lillie's situation. It was all coming together in its own timing. She felt even more determined to get back to her trailer and start writing. Maybe after a nice walk on the beach first. She hopped into her Durango and pulled out into traffic.

⇒ Eighteen ⇐

It was a week later when Kate pressed send on her email to Margaret. She didn't know if it was the salty air, being back home, or both, but she had locked onto her manuscript like a bull rider aiming for a buckle—not letting go until it was complete. Now, she sat back in satisfaction and stretched her neck as she felt the weight of the words and the story slip away. She'd have at least a month before she'd get edits back, which meant she could completely forget about it and set her mind to other things, like visiting with Lillie.

Her phone buzzed with a text: **Got it.**

Kate smiled as she looked forward to hearing what Margaret had to say. As opinionated as she was, Margaret was very good at giving her honest feedback. She also looked forward to hearing what her editor thought.

This being her second fiction novel, she was particularly curious about whether her editor saw an improvement overall in her storytelling or not. This one was harder to write than the first, particularly because she felt the pressure to outperform. She knew that she shouldn't worry, but she did. Every book she wrote, especially the good ones, felt as though they birthed themselves. As if she had no say in the matter and at any moment the magic would disappear. She knew that wasn't true. Well, at least she hoped it wasn't.

She reached for her phone to call Zach and

tell him the good news. He'd been busy trying to get investors together and figure out a new strategy for the winery. She hoped that he'd finally had the breakthrough he'd been praying for.

The call went directly to voice mail, and Kate left a message for him before setting her phone down and deciding to take a walk on the beach. It was a breezy day but sunny, and she loved walking down to watch the surfers try over and over to ride the crest of the waves.

A half hour later, she returned to her trailer to find her phone screen full of bubbles of missed phone calls from Zach. And a text: **Call me.**

Uh-oh. Her gut hummed its warning as she picked up the phone and pressed the button to return his call.

"Kate." Zach answered almost immediately.

"Hey! What's happening? I was just calling to tell you my good news," she sang into the phone.

"At least one of us has good news." He

said, the words coming through a seemingly clenched jaw.

"Oh? What's happened?" Kate asked and sat down in her dinette bench.

"Peter. That's what. Guess what arrived today at the winery?" he asked, and then answered before she could respond. "A pallet with bottles of California wine."

"Oh!" Kate listened.

"That jerk decided to ignore everything I've been telling him for the past few months, and he went ahead and arranged this delivery without my or Dennis's consent." Kate heard the rare current of anger in his normally even voice.

"Why would he do this?" she asked.

"Because he only cares about himself."

"What will you do? I mean, you aren't going to sell it are you?"

"Absolutely not. I refused to accept the delivery, which caused a bit of an issue with the driver, but there is no way I want to be associated with this at all," he fumed. "It's not just the winery; my reputation is at stake here. Fredericksburg is a small town, and all these winery owners I've been working with and telling how invested I am in selling Texas wine will think that I'm full of crap if they find out."

It was the first time Kate had heard him this upset, and except for the circumstances, it excited her. She loved hearing his passion and believed him even more when he was willing to make a stand so strongly like this.

"What are you going to do?" she asked.

"He's gone. We are through. As far as I'm concerned, this is a direct violation of our agreement."

"What does Dennis think?"

Zach cleared his throat. "Dennis didn't like him from the beginning, so he's not going to lose any sleep over this. The frustrating part is that I don't yet have my other investors locked in, so that means there will be a delay in opening the tasting room. If we open it at all."

"Zach, you'll get it open. I know you will." Kate swallowed. "I bet down the road you will thank your stars that you found out about Peter so early. You still have time to bring together the right people to see your vision through."

"Thanks, Kate. And I'm sorry for being so gruff," he apologized. "I just really thought after I traveled out to California the last time that we had an understanding. He totally reneged."

Kate just listened and could only imagine the level of frustration he was feeling at this moment. "It's hard enough to live your own dreams, but even harder when you are fighting against those who are supposed to be on your team."

"You said it," he agreed. "Tell me about your good news?"

Kate perked up. "I just finished my manuscript and sent it off to Margaret!"

"Fantastic! I can't wait to read it, Kate," he said, and she knew he meant it.

"Now, I get to spend a few more days here with Lillie, and then I'll plan to make my way back to Texas, and you," she said sweetly into the phone.

"We both miss you." The tension in Zach's voice had eased up. "I'd better get going, as I have some more calls to make. Let's talk tomorrow?"

"Sounds good. I'll be praying that you get through this and end up in even better shape than before," Kate said before they rang off.

She looked out the rounded window in the front of her trailer just as the sun dropped down below the cliffs to the west. On cue, the sky blossomed in an orange burst as if the sun had set it on fire. She watched as the colors grew more intense, covering the horizon, and marveled at how each time was different. Each time she saw different shades, unique hues. It was a masterpiece she never tired looking at.

⇒ Nineteen ⇐

It was Saturday, and Kate sat on a barstool at the end of the long wooden bar. She watched her sister expertly set up on the small stage in the corner, taking care and precision with each piece of equipment. She felt extremely proud in that moment, thinking about how it had always been Lillie's dream to play music, and now here she was—a talented musician who had toured for three years in France. It had to be satisfying for Lillie to come back home and show folks that she'd done it: she'd achieved her goal and came back to tell.

Kate turned to order another beer, hearing the E string plucked as Lillie tuned her guitar. Being back in the Northwest, she'd slipped into her old habit of drinking IPAs. There was nothing quite like pine-fresh hops poured cold from a tap. She took a long sip off the top, then turned to lean her back against the bar. She had made the decision to head to Texas on Monday. With her manuscript done and Lillie seeming to be getting along fine, she figured it was time for her to get back and see what her own next steps were. She also wanted to spend more time with Zach as he worked toward reaching his own dreams with the winery.

Her time in Port Angeles had been another perfectly unplanned trip. At first, she wasn't sure how much help Lillie would need, but once she'd arrived, she had realized that her sister was managing just fine. Kate had been able to focus and get her manuscript completed on time, and she felt grateful and relieved.

She heard strumming and watched as her sister played like it was second nature. Lillie opened her mouth to sing, and folks at the bar turned around to take notice. Conversations died down as everyone grew mesmerized by her uniquely beautiful voice, equal parts breath and melody.

Kate watched her play, and it was almost as though Lillie was in a trance, bringing everyone with her. At the end of the song, everyone clapped loudly, and Lillie just opened her eyes and smiled in wonder—as if she had forgotten anyone else was in the room. She then picked up her fiddle and began to play haunting melodies and tap out the rhythms with her boots. The same cowboy boots she'd bought in Fredericksburg, the roses wrapped around her ankles.

Two hours and three IPAs later, Lillie finished to applause before the house music came back on the overhead speakers. She joined Kate at the end of the bar and took a long drink from a bottle of water.

"Lillie, that was gorgeous. You've gotten really good since I last heard you play!" Kate gushed.

"Thanks, sis. It was a little weird not playing with Paul or the band, but also kind of nice to be able to just do it on my own." She looked at her older sister. "Sometimes it's nice to not have to worry about others and just focus on yourself, if that makes sense?"

"Oh, yes. That makes total sense." Kate smiled and hugged her.

"Are you ready to head back?" Lillie asked.

"I am. When I first got here, I thought I'd never want to get back out on the highway again. But now I feel the urge to get back..."

"Perhaps, to get back to a certain special someone who adores you?" Lillie teased.

"Perhaps." Kate blushed.

"Do you think you'll ever get married again?" Lillie asked, taking Kate off-guard.

"Well, I don't know...maybe?" She struggled to find how she really felt. "I mean, yes. I want to be married again. I really miss it. But I don't know what it will take for me to trust again."

Lillie nodded, "I understand. For what it's worth, though, you belong back there. With Zach."

Kate looked at her sister, realizing how wise she could be sometimes in spite of her age. "I think you may be right."

"I borrowed Meg's car and drove out to the old house yesterday," Lillie said. "The daffodils are blooming like mad."

Kate chuckled, "Mom sure loved those things. Remember how upset she got when we cut all of them that one spring?"

"Oh, my gosh, I can hear her now. 'Those flowers are meant to be outdoors, not stuck in a vase inside!'" Lillie imitated their mother's voice, and they both fell into laughter.

"Was it weird to be back?" Kate asked her.

"I thought it would be, but actually it was good. I felt at peace about it," Lillie said.

"You know she would be thrilled about your baby," Kate said, giving her sister's arm a squeeze.

"Yeah." Lillie paused for a moment, thinking. "It might be the pregnancy hormones talking, but I can almost feel her here."

Kate nodded and pulled her in for a hug. "She is."

They chatted and laughed until the sun started dropping low and it was time for Kate to head back to the RV park. She didn't like getting back in the dark, and it had been somewhat of a ritual for her to watch the sunset each night.

Lillie walked her out to her Durango, and they hugged on the sidewalk.

"You be safe getting back, OK?" Lillie said.

"Don't worry, I will. And you keep that girl safe." Kate motioned to her sister's belly. "She's lucky to have a momma to sing so sweetly to her."

"She gives me reason to," Lillie said and gave Kate one final squeeze.

As Kate got into the SUV, she leaned out, "Be sure to keep me posted about Paul. I'm rooting for y'all."

"You bet." Lillie smiled and waved, stepping back as Kate fired up the ignition and pulled away from the curb. She looked in the rearview at her sister's image fading behind and felt secure in that moment, knowing that she was going to be just fine. They both would be.

———

IT WAS THE FOURTH night of her trip heading back, the pull of the South strong and comforting. Each day, Kate felt closer to Zach and the rugged landscape of the Hill Country that she'd fallen in love with. It was as though an invisible force was guiding her back toward home: her new home.

Back in Durango, at the foot of the majestic Rocky Mountains, she'd sat outside her Airstream. The night's air was crisp, so she huddled underneath her mother's faded quilt, peering up into the night's sky. The tapestry of stars twinkled brightly with the new moon, and Kate could make out the faint outline of the Milky Way.

A mile high, she shivered with the closeness of the sky, as her eyes wandered from one constellation to another. It was a perfect moment, and she savored it for herself. She thought about how she might share this with Zach in the future. But for now, she needed this time alone.

Alone. She had spent the last year navigating that foreign space until it became comfortable. Now, she needed to open up that universe to include another. It was exciting and terrifying at the same time. Having finally found her voice again, and embracing her new nomadic lifestyle, she was reluctant to be tethered too soon. Or for the wrong reasons. She needed to be sure about him. To be sure that she could maintain her own boundaries while still letting him in. It was a delicate balance, as precarious as the stars hanging in the dark, inky sky. Yet, she knew that they were in perfect balance with each other. Each one had its own weight, gravitational pull, and trajectory. Together, they created a constellation of images for us to navigate by. She spied the three stars anchoring Orion's belt. Lillie, Paul, and the baby? Kate, Zach, and...Chloe? She longed for family and felt the tug between being with Lillie and investing in a future with Zach.

Kate closed her eyes and said a silent prayer for guidance. She prayed for Lillie and the baby. She prayed for Paul. She prayed for Zach's winery. And for Chloe. Then she prayed for herself, that she would find the guidance for her own journey.

She opened her eyes, and the stars silently overwhelmed her senses again. Then she saw a bright flashing light streak in a long arc across the sky. A shooting star! Kate grinned and felt in that instant her prayers were heard.

⇒ Twenty ⇐

Kate woke bathed in sunshine. She breathed in deeply and then exhaled all the ache and fatigue from the long drive. She'd made it back home to the Hill Country. She lingered in bed for a moment, luxuriating in the fact that she didn't need to get up to travel today. It had been another grueling six days, but somehow coming back seemed a shorter distance. Grateful her manuscript was delivered, she now had four weeks to relax before the final copyedits arrived.

Her phone dinged: "Welcome home! Xo"

She smiled and rolled over to call Zach back.

He answered on the first ring. "Kate. I'm so glad you're back."

"Me too. It's amazing to not have a travel day today." She leaned back against her pillows, opening up her back window to the field behind her site.

"What have I missed? What's happening with the winery?" she asked.

"I have good and bad news," Zach said.

"Good news first," Kate replied anxiously.

"After reaching out to some of the other owners that we've cultivated relationships with, I am amazed to say that they have offered us barrels of some of their best wines to bottle and sell to get the tasting room open," he said. "Los Pinos, Messina Hof, Texas Heritage, and Hye Meadow have all offered to help."

"Oh, wow! So, they'll just sell you the wine, and all you have to do is bottle it?" Kate asked.

"Pretty much. We'll be bottling it at Kerrville Hills later this week if you are up for the trip?"

"I wouldn't miss it. I've been really intrigued by this whole business," she said, adding, "See, I told you that it would work out somehow."

"This community is really amazing. I literally couldn't have done it without their help and expertise," he reflected.

"What's the bad news?" She was almost afraid to ask. "Is the business with Peter over?"

"Yes. He's gone," Zach stated. "I was able to get a few smaller silent investors from back in the Northeast, and I think that once we start to build up our wine club, we will have enough support to get this tasting room off the ground."

"OK, good! So?" She prodded him.

"It means we'll be delayed opening the tasting room by a few months now, though, as we need to let the wine mature in the bottles," he said with a heavy voice.

"Well, it could be worse, right?" Kate said, relieved it wasn't. "At least you will still be opening and on your terms. Peter can go back to California!"

"Precisely. It may take us a little longer to get on our feet in terms of being fluid, but I can't tell you how relieved I am that I'm no longer worried about Peter. Just the fact that we will be opening at all is almost a miracle."

"Miracles do come true, Dr. Wine," Kate teased, and heard him chuckle on the other end.

"Indeed, they do, Kate. Although, it may not be the last we see of Peter. I've heard that he's bringing partners out from California to possibly open his own tasting room later this year."

Kate grimaced at the thought, "Well, you just focus on your own vision and don't worry about him."

"It makes me even more proud to be standing by the other owners who have sacrificed to keep Texas wine a viable business. I think that folks will appreciate that story more than buying cheaper wine from out of state," he said.

"They will. Before long, you'll be harvesting your own grapes and making authentic Texas wine. For now, I think this is a great opportunity to lean into the spirit of this community," she said with warmth lacing her voice.

"It's been an incredible process so far. I wouldn't change a thing." He paused for a moment before continuing. "I've got to go, but I'll send you the GPS for Kerrville Hills by text. We'll start at 7 a.m. on Thursday, but feel free to come when you can."

"I'll be there," she said, excited at the idea of her first bottling event. "See you soon!"

They rang off, and Kate was full of pride thinking about how much of a struggle it had been for Zach so far and how gracefully he'd handled it. She looked forward to getting a be-hind-the-scenes look at this wine business and said a prayer of thanks that he'd been able to continue pursuing his dream in spite of the obstacles.

⇀ Twenty-One ↽

It was 9 a.m. when Kate arrived at Kerrville Hills Winery. She pulled through the limestone gate and followed the drive up to the large metal buildings she assumed were the production facility.

She found a parking spot nearby, then cut her engine and stepped out to walk toward the opening. She saw a long, enclosed trailer backed up to one side of the pass-through between the metal buildings and could hear the clanking of bottles and the sounds of a forklift engine scooting back and forth. She stepped past a row of barrels and heard people laughing as they chatted along a conveyor belt that was pushing boxes of bottles down to a makeshift table where two people taped up the bottom of the boxes and then passed them to another who lifted the cases onto a forklift.

She walked a step further and then heard her name over the cacophony. "Kate!" Zach waved at her, and she made her way to where he was standing to the side of a pallet of empty bottles, talking with Dennis and another woman.

Zach moved toward her quickly and enveloped her in a big hug, squeezing her tightly before kissing her lightly on the cheek. "I'm glad you're here," he said, giving her one more squeeze before guiding her back to the group.

"Kate! Great to see you again!" Dennis gave her a warm hug.

"And this is Leah, our winemaker," Zach said as he introduced the woman to Kate.

Leah reached her hand out and shook Kate's. "Pleasure to meet you."

She was wearing a baseball cap that had the red and black Texas Tech emblem on it, with her brown hair wrapped up in a low bun. Her grip was firm and steady, and Kate sensed she was a no-nonsense kind of woman. Kate immediately liked her.

"It's great to meet you, too, Leah," she said.

Kate turned back to all the activity. "So, tell me what's happening."

Zach pointed to a row of barrels to one side of the barn structure. "Those are the barrels we've been able to purchase from various local wineries." Then he pointed inside to a large metal vat. "We put each varietal into this tank and then pump it over in these hoses to the truck that has the bottling equipment."

He walked her over to the truck, and she smiled and nodded at some of the volunteers helping on the line.

"We put the empty bottles here into the machine, and then it feeds through and fills each bottle and corks it. Then we carefully put the bottles back into the cartons, tape them up, and stack them onto the pallets for storage." He pointed out the various stations to her as he talked.

"Wow. So, how many cases of each are you going to bottle?" she asked, taking it all in.

"We started with a Viognier and a Rosé and are now moving into the Tempranillo and Merlot." He pointed to a dry-erase board on the side of the wall. "We have two barrels each, so we are hoping to get about fifty cases, or about six hundred bottles. But that can vary. And of course, we have the burn bottles that cost us a bit of wine."

"Burn bottles?" Kate inquired.

"Yes, when we switch the wine in the tank, the first few cases aren't suitable for sale as they may contain residue of the previous batch of wine. So we call them burn bottles and usually give them to the volunteers for their efforts," he explained and then pointed to a few white cases stacked to one side of the room with the word "BURN" in Sharpie on the side.

"Interesting!" Kate said as Dennis came over to Zach with a couple of plastic cups.

"We just started on the Tempranillo. Try this," he said and handed one to Zach and the other to Kate.

She looked at the rich liquid and brought it up to her nose. She caught a whiff of the cherry aroma and tobacco before taking a sip and letting the wine warm her palate with lingering tannins. "Wow, this is really good!" she said, taking another sip.

Zach nodded in agreement as they eyed each other over their glasses. "Give this another month or two in the bottle, and it will be fantastic."

She watched as the bright red fluid made its

way from the tank to the truck in a long hose. Everyone was busy with a job, and she finished her cup and was anxious to help out. "Where can I start?"

"Well, why don't we give these folks a break?" Zach nodded to the couple taping up the cases. "Y'all want to get a bite to eat?" He said to the volunteers as he motioned inside where cheese and crackers had been set out and some soup in a Crock-Pot was ready to be served.

They agreed, and Kate and Zach took their positions on either side of the table. The next case was passed down quickly, and Zach grabbed it and held the sides of the box together while Kate deftly used the roller with shipping tape to seal it up. Then they passed it down the line and another guy grabbed the case and stacked it on the pallet.

Each case came down quickly, and Kate and Zach worked together like an expert team. She liked it when she had to lean over to tape the box and get that much closer to him. She also liked how easygoing he was with everyone around him, not afraid to roll up his sleeves and help out.

"This is hard work but fun," Kate said, as she took her job seriously and made sure the tape was on just right.

With the next row of cases on the pallet completed and stacked four high, the forklift moved underneath to take them to the storage room while another empty pallet was placed down on the cement floor. This rotation and rhythm of bottling, taping, and lifting soon became second nature. Kate thrilled at the thought of each case soon to be labeled and presented at the tasting room. Just then, she heard a commotion and looked up to see grim faces heading toward the back storeroom. Zach asked one of the volunteers to take over as he went to investigate.

Kate continued taping the cases and

wondered what was going on, when another volunteer came out and asked for towels. Kate quickly said, "I'll take them!" and turned to tag in another volunteer to take over her duty.

She grabbed the stack of towels and made her way to the door that led to the refrigerated storeroom. Stepping around a stack of neatly organized shrink-wrapped cases, she stopped short. In front of her on the floor, were the remnants of a pallet of cases that was all torn asunder. There was broken glass, wine, and damaged boxes strewn all over the cement floor.

"Oh my gosh, what happened?" Kate exclaimed.

Zach turned to her. "A pallet broke," he said very calmly as everyone was taking in the scene.

"I've never seen that happen before," one of the volunteers said and then filled Kate in on what had happened. "As the forklift was stacking one pallet full of shrink-wrapped cases of wine on top of the other, the top pallet broke, crashing down on top of the other. Two pallets of damaged bottles, that could represent over $15K worth of wine if they lost them all." Kate grimaced. She turned to Zach, watching as he turned into doctor mode and began triaging.

"Kate, can you take those towels to Dennis and start pulling out—very carefully—the bottles to see if we can salvage anything. Dennis, if you can continue to cut the boxes open and pass the cases or bottles to Kate, I'll mop up and try to clean up the broken glass. We can toss the damaged boxes over here," he said evenly as he pointed to a corner.

"We can still sell most of these at the tasting room, even if the labels have a little damage. But we need to separate those from the ones that are in good condition as those will go to our Wine Club members," Dennis explained to Kate as she took each bottle, gently wiped it off with a towel, and lined it up with the others to be placed into new cartons.

Leah helped the winemaker extricate the forklift, and they all worked methodically for a few hours until they were able to make their way through all the cases. It was hard to tell how many bottles were damaged as the scene looked so gruesome with red wine, crumpled boxes, and broken glass everywhere.

It wasn't just that they could lose this wine; it was also the fact that they had already gone to great lengths to secure it in the first place. They had called in all their favors and didn't have any extra barrels to supplement. This was their entire yield to kick-start the winery, and they needed every single bottle they could get.

She watched Zach as he swept up the glass and continued to work, extricating the cases out of the shrink-wrap. He was so calm and collected and didn't get angry or raise his voice once. She knew that he likely learned this from his medical training, but she admired him all the more seeing it in action.

Finally, the scene had been cleared, and they began re-casing the good wines and setting aside cases and marking them for the tasting room. Kate couldn't believe it; out of all that destruction, only three cases of wine—thirty-six bottles—were lost. Amazing.

Thank you. We needed that miracle.

They went about restacking the cases and brought in the shrink-wrap, then carefully stacked the pallet on top of the other with the forklift.

Kate grabbed the towels to take to the main room, and Zach gave her a squeeze from behind. "Nice work."

She smiled and leaned into him. "That was scary. This wine business is definitely unpredictable." He nodded in agreement and then grabbed the towels to toss them into a bin.

She wondered at how much he could handle. First, the loss of Peter, then the uncertainty of opening the tasting room, and now almost losing the wine? It seemed like the punches never stopped coming.

She walked over to Dennis at the line with the others and nodded to him in relief that things were OK. Just then she heard, "Walking!" yelled from the tank room.

"What does that mean?" she asked Dennis.

"When we reach the end of the tank, the winemaker 'walks the hose,' getting as much wine to the truck and stopping before the air bubbles."

"Got it," Kate said, impressed with the coordination of the whole effort.

"That's it. We've finished with the Merlot," he said, and everyone high-fived and then started cleaning up their stations as the remaining pallet was shrink-wrapped and moved to the storage room.

Kate went into the main room and poured herself a glass from the open pitchers on the table. The last bits of each barrel that didn't make it in. The Merlot was incredibly delicious, too, silky smooth with a rich jammy flavor.

It wasn't enough for her to just drink and appreciate the wines. She realized in that moment that she wanted to be part of the process. She wasn't sure just how she would do this or what role she would play, but she trusted that it would happen.

She watched as Dennis and Zach handed out the burn bottles and thanked the volunteers. Just then, Zach looked up, caught her eye, and gave her a playful wink. She felt warm all over and grateful that after all the winding roads in her life so far, this is where she had ended up.

⇉ Twenty-Two ⇇

Kate got back into her truck to drive home and saw she had a missed phone call from Lillie and a text message: "call me!!"

She quickly pressed the button to call her sister back, worried that maybe something bad had happened.

"Sis!" Lillie answered breathlessly.

"Are you OK? Is the baby OK?" Kate rushed out, afraid to hear the answer.

"Oh, yes! We are fine! I just have really good

news!" Lillie said and couldn't hold herself back, "I'm getting married!"

"What! Oh my gosh!" Kate said, then added, "To Paul, right?"

"Yes, of course, silly!" Lillie giggled.

"Lillie, this is fantastic news!" Kate let her breath out and looked up to the sky, thinking about her prayers being answered.

"Paul's coming here, and we are thinking of just planning something very small—maybe at Meg and Rick's. We're not sure yet, really." Lillie took a breath. "You know we don't have much of a budget with the baby coming and all."

As Kate listened, an idea shot through her mind. She had a little stashed away from the sales of her last novel, and she was looking for a way to help support the tasting room.

"Wait, what if you come down here to Fredericksburg and have the wedding in Zach's winery?" She asked.

"That would be amazing, but I doubt we can

afford it right now," Lillie said. her sweet voice sounding uncertain.

"My treat," Kate said. "Lillie, this is a big day, and I know Mom would want it to be celebrated properly."

"Really, sis?"

"Absolutely. No question. I'll pay for your flights and all the arrangements." Kate started to grow excited. "Now that my manuscript is off to the copy editor, I have time on my hands. You know that planning parties was one of my favorite activities when I was with David."

"Oh, my gosh. I'm so excited. A Hill Country wedding?" Lillie was elated, and Kate smiled as she heard the joy in her sister's voice.

"Obviously, with the baby coming, we would need to do this soon. How about early April?" Kate asked.

"That's perfect. I'll invite Meg, Rick, and maybe some of our friends from Paris if they can come." Lillie said. "Oh, and Caroline, too!"

"She'd love that. I just need to confirm with Zach, but with the recent setback to opening the tasting room, I think this would be a perfect way to use the space in the meantime," Kate continued. "I'll let you know for sure once I talk with him, OK?"

"This is amazing, sis," Lillie said. "Thank you."

"I'm happy to. We are family," Kate said thinking about how her family was suddenly growing with Lillie, Paul, and the new baby to come. Spring was suddenly blossoming.

They rang off, and Kate quickly dialed Zach's number.

"Miss me already?" he answered.

"Well, of course." Kate blushed. "I have a business proposition for you."

"I'm all ears."

"What if I were to plan a private wedding at the tasting room in early April, bringing in some additional revenue while the doors are closed?" she asked, swallowing as she waited for his answer.

"I hadn't thought about using it as a private event space," he said thoughtfully. "That actually would help out a lot. Who's wedding?"

Kate practically squealed, "Lillie's!"

"What? Oh, Kate, that's amazing! So she and Paul figured things out?" Zach said with relief in his voice.

"Yes. I am thrilled for them both. They wanted to do something small back up in Port Angeles, but I convinced her that a Hill Country wedding would be the perfect way to celebrate." She added, "And at Winsome Winery!"

He laughed. "Kate, I love the idea. Go for it. Just let me know if you need any help planning or connecting with folks. I'm happy to help."

"Thank you! I'd better get planning!" she said and rang off after they said quick goodbyes.

Lillie's wedding. At Zach's winery. Kate

shivered in excitement as she started thinking about ideas for decorating. She pushed down the pedal on her Durango and sped up toward home so she could get started.

⇒ Twenty-Three ⇐

The next day, Kate sat at her dinette table in her Airstream. Her laptop displayed glowing Pinterest inspiration boards, and she was writing out ideas on pieces of paper as she spoke with Lillie over the phone.

"How about we keep this simple but elegant?" Lillie began. "I love the woodwork at the winery and figure we can just add some nice touches with white ribbons, and then of course contrast that with the purplish-blues of the bluebonnets."

Kate agreed. "Yes, and thick candles in hurricane lamps, with strings of white lights hanging throughout."

Lillie hummed with delight. "Oh, yes. I mean, I think we should do this as a sunset wedding, don't you think? This way the lights will make it all that much more romantic as they hang from the oak tree in the back patio?"

Kate knew exactly what her sister wanted. "It helped that you sent me your Pinterest board of ideas. I am going to run around and see if I can't find all the decor locally first, and then I'll order anything that we can't find. What about cake? Did you want something tiered? Formal?"

"I'm not too picky about that. What do you think we should do?" Lillie asked her.

"Well, we are having this Hill Country-themed wedding in Fredericksburg. What about German chocolate cake? Or maybe pecan tarts?" Kate asked.

"Oh, both would be really delicious and

unique. Paul and I eat anything, so you can feel free to surprise us. Obviously, budget is the issue, so we'll have to keep that in mind. I'm not sure how much it will cost us to cater this, and it looks like just ten or twelve people coming, so whatever you come up with will work for us."

Kate smiled as she knew exactly the chef to cater this event. A month ago, she had attended a tasting at Ab Astris Winery, where the chef paired some of their finest wines with his uniquely inspired creations. She would see what he'd charge to do this small event and whether he could pair the food with Winsome wines instead.

"I'm on it, sis." She grinned and then jotted down a few notes on the blank piece of paper in front of her.

"Of course, entertainment is taken care of. Paul and I are putting together a special set list. It will be wonderful to perform together again," Lillie said.

"I can't wait to hear you two." Kate smiled as she imagined them playing on the side of the patio and how beautiful his guitar and her fiddle would sound.

"OK, I think I've got everything I need for now. I'm going to make some calls, and I'll be back in touch with you with any questions," Kate said.

"Thanks, sis! Also, we should probably plan to come out a few days early to stay before the wedding and help set everything up," Lillie said.

"Yes, I was just going to suggest the same. I checked with my friends at the Stonewall Motor Lodge, and they've agreed to a block of rooms for that week. Once you know for sure, call them to book. I'll text you their link."

"OK, I'll book our flights and send you the details once that's confirmed. Paul's parents are flying in from France, so I'll try to get them rooms as well." She breathed anxiously into the phone. "I can't believe how soon this is all happening!"

"Sis, don't worry. I'm going to take care of everything on my end You just focus on growing that beautiful baby."

"She's growing all right, I've been eating like a horse!" Lillie thanked her sister again before ringing off.

Kate spent the next few hours calling around to coordinate all the things they had discussed. She had to leave some messages but was able to check off many of the items on her list. She loved to plan and throw events. It was one of the things that she had enjoyed about being married to a celebrity of sorts. She could entertain all of David's artistic friends and had a special way of making everything just right. It was all about the little touches. The details.

Kate knew from experience that you didn't need a lot of money to throw a really nice party. She was crafty and already had some ideas in mind about how she would hang beautiful crys-tal-like orbs from the branches of the oak tree and make her own ribbon decor from spools she would find at a craft store.

When she lived in the house with David, she'd had storage bins full of decor for any occasion. Now, of course, she didn't have any room for storage and had relinquished much of her stock in the divorce.

Never mind. Kate was determined to hit every store to find just the perfect touches that represented Lillie and Paul's love.

Now that she had a few weeks before her edits were back, she could plunge full-time into this excursion, and she couldn't wait to get started.

She glanced up at the clock: 3:45 p.m.

Mentally calculating, she knew it would be after four by the time she drove to the nearest shops at Bee Cave. Probably not worth trying to navigate rush-hour traffic. Instead, she made a detailed list for herself and planned to leave early the next morning to hunt for all the items.

She poured herself another glass of wine and then sat back, satisfied in her plan. If all went well, she would have all the items in a few days. She didn't know what was more exciting: shopping for herself or for someone else. Certainly, she loved the hunt for the special deals and loved seeing what she could put together on her shoestring budget.

She wondered what Paul's parents would be like. Would they expect something more lavish? Or at a church? Shoot! She realized she had forgotten to ask Lillie about that part. They were planning to pick up the marriage certificate at the courthouse but would need someone to officiate the wedding.

Kate believed in the vows of matrimony, and she believed in having God's blessing. She did not, however, think that this had to take place within a church. They weren't affiliated with any of the local churches and probably couldn't afford the cost anyway.

No, she felt that a wedding out in the open with her family and friends close by would be a wedding God would approve of. It was a miracle in itself that Lillie and Paul had come together. She knew that as a couple they would raise their baby in the best way they knew how.

As Kate pondered this, her phone rang: Zach.

"How's my favorite author and Texas wine lover?" his voice came sweetly over the line.

"Well, you can add wedding planner to that list now." she laughed.

"You are a woman of many talents," he responded warmly.

"Aw, shucks." Kate grinned to herself. "I may have some questions about sourcing wine for the wedding party to pair with the dinner. Do you mind?"

"Not at all. In fact, that's why I was asking. I have two cases set aside for you, and if

I can swing it, I'll have them labeled special just for the wedding with Paul and Lillie's names on them."

"Oh! That will be perfect!" Kate said excitedly as she checked that box on her list.

"When are you planning to be back in Fredericksburg?" he asked.

"Well, I think by the end of the week, I'll plan to come out and start pre-setting some things at the tasting room to be sure I'm not forgetting anything for Lillie's wedding. I'm hoping to get most of the decor in the next few days, and then I'll be back to meet the catering crew in person and firm up any other details," Kate said. "I can't believe how close it is, that my sister will be back out here in a matter of weeks!"

"Yeah, this year is really flying by. Chloe is really excited to help out with the wedding too," he said. "I'm so proud of her. She's doing great in school and really loving it. I thought at first she'd miss the Northeast a little, but so far she has taken to it like a duck to water."

"What a relief! That would be horrible if you planned this whole winery life, and she hated Texas," Kate said.

"You know I wouldn't let that happen," Zach said playfully. "I know you are busy with the wedding right now, but I'm planning on heading out to look at our vines in the Hill Country AVA near the end of the week. Would you like to join me?"

"I'd love to!" Kate grew excited. "I've been wanting to get a better look at the vines and learn more about growing. In fact, maybe I'll hitch up and stay local for the weekend so I'll have more time to decorate the tasting room."

"And see a certain someone as well?" Zach teased.

Kate laughed, "Of course! That was a given."

"It's a date." Zach said.

Kate grinned in anticipation. "I'd better get back to Lillie's preparations. I'll text you later?"

"You bet. Talk later."

Kate loved getting to be more hands on with the wine business. Lillie's wedding, vineyard visits, and springtime in Fredericksburg? She very nearly pinched herself.

Instead, she decided to get rid of some of her energy and take a walk around the RV park. She put on her New Balance sneakers, grabbed a ball cap, then stepped out of her trailer and into the windy and warm air outside. As she began to pick up her stride, she breathed deeply and let it out, striding forward with a steady pace.

⇛ Twenty-Four ⇚

The next morning, Kate woke up early and made her coffee in a travel mug before revving up her engine and heading out of the park. She wound her way around the usual hills and noticed that the landscape was beginning to change colors with the coming spring. The browns gave way to yellows, and she could see a few bluebonnets begin to dot the side of the highway. Springtime in Texas—soon, the hills would be vibrant with colors.

She was flicking through her console to

find some music to play when she saw Caroline calling.

"Well, hello there, friend!" she chirped into her speaker as she navigated the roadway.

"Guess who just booked her flight to Texas?" Caroline sang into the phone.

"Yay! I can't wait to see you!" Kate cheered.

"I wouldn't miss this wedding for the world. And besides, I've been dying to meet Dr. Wine." Caroline's voice came out dripping like syrup.

"He's worth the wait." Kate laughed at her own joke. "I just spoke with Lillie yesterday, and she's booking rooms at the motor lodge. I think I'll camp out with my trailer there too. Let me see if we can snag a room or cabin for you too."

"That would be lovely, darlin'! Do you need me to bring anything?" Caroline asked.

"I think I've got everything set. I just need you!" Kate said.

"All righty! Just keep me posted." Caroline said before ringing off.

Kate looked up the number to Stonewall Motor Lodge and dialed it while keeping her eye on the road. Ten minutes later, she was able to secure an RV spot for herself and a cabin for her dear friend. The traffic in Bee Cave was picking up, so she waited until she was parked in front of Michaels to text Caroline with the good news.

For the next hour, Kate made her way in and out of the shops: Home Goods, Michaels, and World Market. She was focused on finding those perfect touches for the wedding decor that would really make the tasting room sing. She then headed to Lowe's and picked up the outdoor hanging lights that she and Zach had agreed on, which would stay permanently in place once the tasting room opened.

Famished, she took a break and grabbed a bite to eat at Panera while going through her list and checking things off. She knew there were a few home-decor stores in Fredericksburg where she hoped to pick up the hurricane lamps and some other local touches of flair.

Her phone buzzed, and a bubble lit up with a link to Caroline's itinerary. Kate marveled at how quickly everything was coming into place. She still needed to firm up the menu, and she called and left a message for the caterer before finishing her lunch and heading back out.

She realized as she got outside, looking at the various clothing boutiques, that she had nothing to wear to her sister's wedding. That certainly wouldn't do!

Kate poked in and out of some stores but didn't find exactly what she needed. She then headed towards Dillard's and made her way to the dress department. She wanted something elegant but comfortable. An understated cocktail dress.

She searched through every rack, hangers clanging against each other as she inspected each dress. Too many sequins. Too short. Too long. Too much neckline. Sleeves too long. On and on she flipped through each hanger until she spied something a few hangers ahead. Just the very top of the hanger had a purplish-pink silk ribbon and a single rhinestone button. She flicked the others out of the way and revealed the rest of the dress.

A beautiful silk halter-top dress that gathered gently around the waist and then opened out to an A-line that ended just above the ankle. It was classic, understated, and absolutely gorgeous. She knew it would look amazing with the bluebonnets on the tables, and she could also dress it up with some of her jewelry already in the trailer.

Hurriedly, she grabbed her size and made her way to the dressing room. Once inside, she put the gown on carefully and then turned around to look at herself in the mirror. She gasped. It was made for her. Standing on tiptoes to imitate heels, she turned around to the left and right, admiring the view. Amazing how the right dress could completely transform a body.

She smiled at herself in the long mirror and nodded. This would be the perfect dress for the maid of honor. And she couldn't wait for Zach to see her in it.

She found a register and purchased the dress before heading for the shoe department. *Let's face it. I'm a glamper now,* she thought. She didn't have any heels anymore. Nope. And this dress demanded heels.

She tried on different options but settled for a pair of nude four-inch leather pointed heels. There was something about putting on heels that gave a sense of authority and poise. She enjoyed walking around the shoe room to be sure there were no pain points (other than the obvious one of them being heels). That decision made, she paid, stepped out of Dillard's and back into her Durango.

Phew! Shopping is exhausting. She put the

Durango into drive so she could head back toward her trailer. She had found everything she could in Bee Cave, and the next mission would take her to downtown Fredericksburg.

Once back at the RV park, she prepared her trailer for the move to Fredericksburg in the coming days. She kept some items in the back of her SUV for delivery to the tasting room and then secured other items inside the trailer for travel.

Kate carefully hung the dress inside the locker in her trailer. She set the box with the heels inside securely as well. Grinning to herself, she was thrilled at the idea of getting dressed up again and couldn't wait to see what Zach looked like in his suit and tie.

She texted him: "Wait until you see what I'll be wearing at the wedding..."

A few moments later she saw the animated gray bubbles. "You are beautiful no matter what you wear."

She laughed at how much of a gentleman he was. "See you tomorrow! xo"

The response came quickly. "Can't wait. XX"

She then realized she didn't know what Lillie would be wearing. She quickly texted her: "What about your dress?"

"I'm bringing it!" Lille answered.

Kate "hearted" the message and then clicked her phone off. She poured herself a glass of Merlot before going through her list again and making a few more notes of places to check in downtown Fredericksburg.

Just then, the chef called, and she talked with him for about an hour as she explained what she wanted and he gave her some options. "This all sounds perfect. I'll drop a check with the deposit off at your tasting room tomorrow afternoon if that's all right?" He agreed, and they rang off.

Checking that item off the list, Kate noted she still had a few unresolved items; she needed

to source the bluebonnets and get cases of sparking and flat water, and she still needed to find
someone to officiate the wedding. Otherwise,
she was making great progress. It was always
a little anxiety-producing until all the pieces
came together and she started setting up for
the event. This was even more so, as it was
Lillie's wedding and she wanted everything to
be just perfect.

Yet, Kate also loved to bring in the element
of fate. Trusting that she would find the right
items and decor and that, just like the dress,
everything would come together as it should
without her needing to control every single
thing. She had learned from the past few years
that the more she leaned into the flow of life,
the more she was met with magical surprises
that made living all the more worthwhile.

She grinned in satisfaction as she looked up
to take another sip of wine and watch the sun
slowly setting over the hills. The sky turned to a

magnificent watercolor of purple, pink, yellow, and orange, and she realized it was very close to the color of the fabric of her dress. A few impatient stars poked through the rich tapestry, and she marveled as the colors deepened until they disappeared completely.

⇒ Twenty-Five ⇐

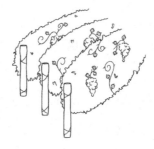

Kate hitched up her trailer and made good time the next morning. As she passed the tiny town of Hye and the vineyards that lined Highway 290, she smiled to herself, remembering dancing with Zach at Hye Meadow a year ago, right before Chloe got into her accident. It seemed like ages ago now.

Just after ten, she arrived at the Limestone Charm RV Park. Situated conveniently off Ranch Road 1376, this new boutique park had only twelve spots, each with beautiful pergolas and picnic benches. Kate pulled into spot number four, unhitched, and connected the water and electric lines. She tested everything before getting back into her Durango and heading up the road.

Driving farther along, she checked her GPS. She had punched in the location of the vineyard where she would be meeting Zach off Grapetown Road, just a mile up the way.

Zach had told her that he'd invested in some Tempranillo grapes from this vineyard to supplement their yield from the High Plains AVA, and he was excited to visit these vines. She slowed down and flicked her blinker on as the GPS told her to turn right.

The paved road grew more narrow and wound around through beautiful farmland with longhorn cattle and goats grazing contentedly alongside the road. At certain points, she would slow down and yield to allow oncoming trucks to pass, as there wasn't enough space for two-way traffic. She dipped down to a water culvert and then back up a short hill as she continued on past picturesque homesteads with fences and metal security gates. Finally, around the next bend, the scenery opened up, and she saw the prominent gray-and-white barn structure of Texas Heritage Vineyard appear majestically off to the right in the distance. It looked magnificent set against the freshly mowed fields with the rows of vines stretching up the hill beyond.

She pulled in through the front gates and drove around the gravel driveway to the side of the main structure, then parked next to Zach's Range Rover.

As she got out, she saw a huge white-and-brown longhorn steer just yards from her on the other side of the fence. He gave her a nod as he continued chewing and turned his head away, seemingly unimpressed. She walked toward the main building and could see a huge open space connecting the two large barn structures and then a second smaller one next door. She walked toward the open space and saw tall rows of barrels stacked to one side, some stacked pallets, and a large piece of equipment.

Rounding the corner, she saw Zach and Dennis in the tank room talking to each other.

"Howdy!" she called and waved as they walked over to give her a hug.

"Welcome! We were just about to head up to look at the vines, so this is perfect timing," Zach said as Leah and the other winemaker came around the corner and motioned to them to jump into his 4WD cart to head up the hill.

Leah was in front, with Dennis, Zach, and Kate in back. The cart took off toward the vineyards, and Kate held on as they navigated the bumpy terrain. They plowed through fields with long grass and weeds before arriving at the first row of vines. The winemaker pointed out the varietals planted, and Kate noticed that each end post had a different color.

They rode along the ten-foot-wide spaces between the vines. A few rows over she saw workers methodically pruning the cordons on the wire. "That's the Montepulciano, a late-blooming varietal that still needs some pruning," the winemaker said as he turned at the end of the row and went up another, and Kate marveled at how peaceful the cordons looked outstretched in surrender.

"This block here is Tempranillo and will be where your yield comes from," he said and abruptly stopped the cart, killing the engine. The quiet overcame Kate, and she could instantly hear the sounds of birds and a mower in the distance. They all hopped out and made their way to begin inspecting the vines.

"Bud break!" Zach exclaimed excitedly as the winemaker pointed out the distance between the green buds coming off the cordon. "We'll keep an eye on these and be cutting back buds to be sure we have an even distribution per foot, but we don't want to make that decision just yet in case there is a late frost."

Leah asked the winemaker a few questions while they continued walking the row. Kate gently touched the newly emerging buds. They looked so hopeful against the dark unyielding texture they came from. She watched the winemaker inspect each vine and explain, "At this point we are just looking for any signs of deficiency, like magnesium, where the vines would turn yellow. So far they are looking good."

They continued inspecting row after row, and Kate grew excited. There was something so magical about farming. Planting something, waiting through the dead of winter, and then beginning to see the signs of new growth. A signal that soon the weather would change and the cordons would be full of large green leaves and beautiful clusters of grapes in different colors.

At that moment, Kate realized the absurdity of something she had taken for granted her whole life: the fact that we associate the color purple with "grape," when in fact grapes can be green, pale yellow, red, and purple.

Having completed their mission, they all got back into the cart and headed back down the hill toward the barns. The view coming down from the vines was truly breathtaking. "This wouldn't be such a bad view to wake up to every day," she said to Dennis, and he nodded in agreement.

"Definitely not." He grinned at her as they held on while the cart bumped back and forth in the ruts on the dirt road.

Back down on the flats, the cart was parked, and they all piled out. Zach and Dennis asked a few more questions about preparing for the upcoming harvest and how many barrels they could expect to yield this season.

"We're hoping you'll have about one ton of

grapes, so that could be anywhere from two to three barrels. We'll just have to see their condition when they come off the vines," the winemaker said. "Of course, it all depends on the weather between now and then. Hang on just a sec." He grabbed a few plastic cups and made his way to one of the large metal tanks.

Opening a valve, he poured out a straw-colored wine into their glasses before bringing it over for them to taste. "This is a blend of Roussanne and Viognier that we are tweaking before bottling. It's called the Time Traveler." They swirled, sniffed, and sipped. Kate tasted the honey, tangerine, and floral notes, as the light wine finished with a mineral texture.

"It's very clean and crisp," she said, as the four of them nodded and compared tasting notes before thanking the winemaker and heading out to their vehicles.

"Y'all want to grab a bite before calling it a day?" Dennis asked.

Kate turned to him. "Sure, I don't have any plans."

"I've got to get back, but I'll talk to y'all later," Leah said before turning to Kate, "It's great to see you again."

"You too!" Kate said and shook her hand again before Leah got into her pickup.

"How about we go to Alamo Springs?" Dennis suggested to Zach and Kate.

"That sounds perfect. Why don't you ride with me, and I'll drop you back here after?" Zach asked Kate.

She agreed and got in on the passenger side.

They drove back along the winding roads, and just as it seemed they were in the middle of nowhere, they came on the Alamo Springs Café. "Best burgers around," Zach said as he pulled up underneath a large oak tree and cut the engine. Dennis pulled in beside them, and they all got out and made their way up the porch to order.

Three Texas-size burger orders later, with various toppings, they headed out to the patio to sit with some cold beers. The joint was popping, and Kate marveled that perhaps "you build it, they will come," actually comes true.

"So Kate, how are you adjusting to your new RV and wine life?" Dennis asked her before he took a long pull off his bottle.

"It's been really amazing," she said. "If you had told me a year ago that this is what I'd be doing—living full time in a sixteen-foot travel trailer and learning about wine in the Hill Country—I would have called you crazy." She laughed. "Somehow, though, it just feels right. It fits."

Dennis nodded. "That's what happens. Folks come out here, like this guy"—he nodded to Zach—"then they get the bug and can never leave."

Zach laughed. "Yeah. I've definitely been bit hard."

She took another sip of her beer and let the cold bubbles rush her throat. "It's been really fun getting to know the area as I plan Lillie's wedding. Folks are really nice here."

"Perhaps you'll find inspiration for your next book?" Dennis asked.

Kate shrugged, "Stranger things have happened."

"How's Lillie's wedding coming anyway?" Dennis asked.

"Great! The only thing is that I'm having a hard time finding someone to officiate on such short notice," Kate said.

Zach raised his eyebrow and jerked his thumb at Dennis. "Looks like you've come to the right place."

"Even a blind hog finds a truffle." Dennis laughed deep in his belly.

Kate was confused, looking back and forth between the two.

"Heck, girl, I was an ordained minister

before I got into the business of wine making," Dennis said.

"You're kidding!" Kate brightened.

"Nope, and seeing as how you are now family, I would be honored to officiate." He pointed the tip of his bottle to hers, and she met him halfway to clink the necks together.

"Wait until Lillie hears this. How perfect!" Kate said. "Thank you, Dennis!"

He brushed it off kindly, and then they settled in to enjoy their burgers. There wasn't a whole lot of talking; just a great deal of satisfaction and licking of fingers.

Kate finished the last pull from her beer bottle before tossing everything into the trash as they made their way out front.

"See you in a few weeks!" Kate said and gave Dennis a great big bear hug. He returned the favor, and she knew that he would be the perfect person to marry her baby sister.

They waved goodbye, and Zach and Kate

headed back to Grapetown Road to drop off Kate at her Durango. It had been a fantastic day. She had visited vines and learned more about growing, her belly was full with maybe one of the best burgers she'd ever had, and she'd ticked off the last box on her wedding checklist. She couldn't imagine anything more perfect until Zach leaned over to kiss her goodbye with sweet and salty lips. Mission accomplished.

Twenty-Six

Two days before the wedding...

Kate was outside on the patio of the Winsome Winery tasting room hanging up the last of the decorations when Zach came in.

"Wow, Kate! This looks amazing!" he exclaimed as he took in the whole scene.

She had woven white lights around the tree trunk of the old oak tree in the center of the patio, then let the lights trail down the branches, dripping romantically. Large and small paper cutout 3D stars hung down randomly, creating a stunning effect.

"I'm just glad I have had enough time to prepare and get everything set up just right," Kate declared as she stood back to admire her handiwork. "Do you think it's too much?"

"Not at all," Zach said, sidling up behind her and wrapping his arms around her. "I think it's creative and festive. Heck, maybe we'll keep them up year round?"

"Well, for sure the café lights will stay up." She pointed to the long strands of black rope that hung overhead above the patio tables at just the right spacing to allow dimmed lighting while still allowing the stars to peek through.

"Those suckers were a pain to hang!" She laughed and turned around to him to snuggle a little closer. "Tell me, Doc. Does this put you in the mood?" She giggled as he pulled her closer, his breath warm as his lips found hers.

Just then, her phone rang in her pocket.

She opened her eyes and reluctantly pulled back. "Sorry! They've probably landed," she said as she fetched her phone from her back jeans pocket to answer.

"Hello?" She wasn't sure whether it was Lillie and Paul, or Caroline, as they were arriving around the same time, but coming from different parts of the country.

"We're here! I'm in line for the rental car, and Paul's fetching our luggage," Lillie said, catching her breath.

"Wonderful! How was your flight?" Kate asked as Zach gently patted her behind before giving her a wink and heading back inside the tasting room.

"It wasn't bad at all. We chatted most of the way, and I got a little nap in, too, so I'm ready for the drive."

"Great! You're just about an hour away from the motor lodge. Text me when you get settled," Kate said.

"Will do. See you soon!" Lillie rang off.

Kate put her phone back into her jeans pocket and then looked at her work so far. At the center of each table was a large Mason jar wrapped with a delicate off-white satin ribbon, just waiting for the bunches of bluebonnets that Kate would be picking up the morning of the wedding.

Surrounding each jar were candle votives and limestone rocks. She wanted to use the native elements as much as possible, and the warm hues of the stones looked perfect set against the clear glass and off-white candles.

She had tried to keep the decorations as simple as possible and yet still make it feel special and unique. The couple would say their vows in front of the oak tree under the canopy of lights. Then the newly wed couple would go to a raised platform at the end of the patio, where they would set up to play their music for their friends and family.

It was going to be a very intimate affair. Caroline from Pensacola. Meg and Rick flying in from Seattle. Paul's parents coming in from France. Dennis and Leah. Chloe and a college friend. And, of course, Zach.

Her phone rang again. This time it must be Caroline.

"Hello, my dear friend!" she sang into the phone.

"The eagle has landed, so to speak. My, it's been too long since I've flown. I forgot how much rigmarole there is with security and liquids. But the good news is that I made it!"

"Wonderful! You may run into Lillie at the rental center, as she just arrived as well." Kate had offered to pick up her friend, but Caroline insisted that she get a car. Kate was honestly relieved since she still had so many last-minute touches to finish before they all had dinner that evening.

"Oh, wouldn't that just be a kick!" Caroline

laughed. "OK, I'm going to fetch my bags and make my way there. I can't believe I'm finally in your great state of Texas. I can't wait to get the whole tour."

"I'm thrilled! I texted you the address to the motor lodge again, and let me know when you get in. Drive safe," Kate said.

"Tootle-oo!" Caroline sang and rang off.

Kate took one more look at the patio and then turned to head back inside the tasting room. "You know, I do believe everything is coming together after all," Kate said partially in disbelief, as Zach poured her a generous glass of Tempranillo.

"And why wouldn't it? I mean, you're now one of the premier wedding planners in Fredericksburg." He winked at her and then filled up his own glass.

"Right." She rolled her eyes and took a sip. "I'm just glad that everyone has made it in so far safely." She paused and fingered the stem of the glass. "It's one thing to plan an event, but there are so many details that could go wrong."

"Yes, but you are a master at handling the unexpected."

"I could say the same of you." She raised her glass to his. "It is fun to see how it's all come together on such short notice. I am so glad that we were able to get the wine cellar at Pontotoc for tonight's dinner. It will be a perfect, intimate way to meet Paul and for everyone to get acquainted."

"I'm looking forward to it as well," Zach said. "I'm going to meet up with Chloe at Hill and Vine. You're welcome to join us."

"Oh no, but thanks. I'm going to head back to the trailer to change, and then Caroline and I will get there a little early to be sure everything is set up. They always do such a fabulous job, though, that likely we'll just be sitting by the fire catching up and waiting for y'all to come." She smiled at him and gave his arm a squeeze.

He locked up the tasting room, and then they kissed goodbye before parting ways.

⇒ Twenty-Seven ⇐

Back at the motor lodge, Kate pulled in front of her trailer and then jumped out. She could see lights on in the cabin where Caroline was staying, and she went up the porch steps and knocked on the door.

Caroline opened and squealed, "I was just about to dial you!" She moved forward and enveloped Kate in a big bear hug. Kate breathed in her Chanel perfume as they held each other tight.

Finally, Caroline pulled back. "What an adorable place this is!"

"Right? It's one of my favorite places to stay, and I sort of like that it's a bit out of Fredericksburg and all the traffic," Kate said as she let herself into Caroline's cabin.

"I've been in the main rooms, but I haven't seen the cabins. This is really cute!" Kate walked around and marveled at all the little touches the owners had added to make the place all the more inviting.

Caroline stepped back over to her bed where her large suitcase was open and began pulling out outfits to hang up. "I couldn't decide what to wear, so I brought a little of everything."

Kate sat down on the edge of the bed as she marveled at her friend's organization. "Well, tonight is casual. And dress with layers because it gets surprisingly chilly once the sun goes down."

"Gotcha. I didn't see Lillie. Did she make it

in?" Caroline asked as she pulled her toiletries out and made her way to the bathroom.

"Yup, she and Paul are resting and then they'll meet us at the restaurant. I figured it would be nice for us to have some one-on-one time before anyway," Kate said.

"I'm still trying to figure out what to get her for a wedding gift. Cash seemed a bit tacky?" Caroline said.

"Well, I bet you'll think of something now that you're here. Besides, you coming is gift enough." Kate said squeezing her friend's arm.

"Well, that is true." Caroline laughed.

"I'm going to get changed, and I'll meet you outside in five?" Kate said as she made her way to the door.

"You bet!" Caroline called out behind her.

Throughout the entire drive back to town, Kate and Caroline caught up as old friends do. They picked up their usual banter and filled each other in on all the particulars: Rob, the kids, Caroline's parents, Pensacola, Zach, the winery, bottling, her book, decorating for Lillie's wedding. Too soon, they arrived at the end of Main Street where Pontotoc was, and Kate pulled in back to park.

They made their way into the courtyard, and Caroline swooned at the scenery. "Oh, my gawd! Look at this adorable sign," she gushed as she made her way around to the front of the old building to take it all in. "Kate, this is like stepping back in time. I love it."

"Me too. It's really one of my favorite places on Main Street because it's got that old-world German charm. The building dates back to 1846." Kate led Caroline past the fires blazing in the courtyard to the steps that led down into the cellar.

Through opened dark-wooden cellar doors and down centuries-worn stone steps, they landed in the small cellar room. The walls on one side were sandstone with dark logs protruding through. In the center of the room stood a long red table with wooden seats all around. Everything seemed to be comfortably worn and beckoned them to stay awhile. The tabletop was set with silverware and cloth napkins, and there were tall candlesticks in the center that glowed brightly.

The owner came down and greeted them both with a bottle and a couple of small Mason jar glasses. While pouring them each a generous glass, he said brightly, "Just let me know when the rest of your party gets here," then headed back up the stairs to wait on the tables in the courtyard.

Caroline and Kate toasted and then settled into the comfortable chairs and let the cozy ambiance take over.

"I feel as though I'm somewhere in Europe," Caroline said as she sipped from her glass.

"I like that it has that romantic sophistication without being pretentious." Kate smiled over her glass at her friend. The candlelight made her friend's features look all the more glamorous. Caroline had a full, beautiful face, with gorgeous lips and a smile that could light up a room.

Kate always felt a tiny bit self-conscious at first, being around someone so comfortable in the space they inhabit. Yet, over time, she'd learned to quickly let it go. Caroline didn't flaunt it, and Kate knew there wasn't any competition.

They both heard footsteps on the stairs and watched as Lillie appeared with a tall, thin, and very striking young man with dark hair right behind her. Lillie was glowing, and her belly was more prominent underneath her red-and-white striped sundress.

"Lillie!" Kate got up and hugged her sister close before Lillie pulled back smiling.

"Kate, this is Paul." Kate looked at the two of them standing together, and she felt instantly that it was right.

"It's a pleasure to meet you, Paul!" she said and pulled him into a hug.

"*Enchant*é." He delicately brushed both of her cheeks with a kiss before pulling away.

Kate had forgotten about this French custom, and she delighted in it. Paul turned to Caroline, and as they were being introduced, Chloe came bounding down the stairs.

"There's the lovebirds!" she giggled and came around to give Lillie a big hug and kiss on the cheek. Zach came down after her and made his way to Kate to give her a kiss before hugging Lillie as well and then firmly shaking Paul's hand.

"Oh, now Dr. Wine, you'd best come over here. It's about time I meet you!" Caroline pushed back her chair to bring him into a huge hug, and Zach eyed Kate over her shoulder, blushing slightly.

"Well, Caroline, I have to say it's a pleasure finally meeting you," Zach said.

"It's about time! Without me, you and this lovely lady"—she motioned her head toward Kate without taking her hands off his shoulders—"would never have met! I think that's worth a bottle of wine or two."

"At the very least." He winked and they all laughed.

They all found their seats and settled in around the table while the owner came down with a tray of glasses and another bottle of wine to pour for everyone. He then disappeared, and they all took a moment to toast the occasion.

Kate kicked it off, "To my dear sister, Lillie, and her wedding to Paul!" They clinked glasses around, and then the conversation picked up with everyone getting to know each other.

As they were talking, the owner brought down trays that had all sorts of delightful goodies: locally made loaves of sourdough bread, jars with homemade spicy pimento cheese, dried meats, rosemary candied pecans, and the owner's specialty brownies. It was served family style, and everyone helped themselves as the conversation continued to flow.

Chloe sat next to Lillie, and they seemed to be deep in conversation. Lillie had told Kate that she and Chloe had been in touch while she'd been away, and that made Kate happy for them both. They were both so young, creative, and passionate. Paul sat on the other side of Lillie, intently listening, while he draped his long arm around her back and delicately brushed her arm every now and then.

They seemed so happy and in love. Kate was thrilled.

Meanwhile, Caroline was deep in conversation with Zach, which honestly made Kate a little nervous. Her friend could be a bit much sometimes, especially when she'd had a few. But Zach smiled broadly and laughed aloud as Caroline grew more animated. He seemed to take it all in stride.

"So, when are your parents getting here, Paul?" Kate asked him as she ripped off a piece of sourdough bread and dipped it in the pimento cheese.

"Tomorrow," he said with his thick French accent. "I will pick them up at the airport."

"Wonderful. I can't wait to meet them," Kate said. She felt for a moment almost like she was standing in for her parents. In a way, she was. Lillie had no other family, and Kate felt that deep sense of purpose and responsibility to watch over her.

"They look forward to meeting you as well." He grinned and squeezed Lillie's arm. "And Lillie, too, of course." He leaned over and kissed his fiancée sweetly on the lips. Lillie's eyes sparkled in the candlelight as she looked lovingly up at him.

Caroline broke away from her interrogation of Zach to join in the conversation. "Tell us about your parents, Paul." She raised her glass and then took a long sip.

"Well, they are from, eh, outside Paris. Mm... in the Bourgogne region," he said, and the pauses to translate each word from French to English were adorable.

"Ah! So, they must know good wine too?" Zach grew interested.

"*Oui*. Our family has some vines but nothing too extravagant," he said, shaking his head. "They mainly lease the land for other winemakers as they do not have the time or energy to work it properly."

"I can't wait to talk with them more about this," Zach said. "The Burgundy region is so rich with history. I hope we are able to impress them with our Texas wines on their visit."

"Do not worry," Paul reassured him. "Although the French are known to be opinionated, my parents are very loving and forgivable."

"Forgiving," Lillie corrected him, patting his hand gently.

"Wow. I want to go to France," Chloe said as she took a bite of brownie and some of the crumbs fell onto the table. "I would die to study photography there. All that history, architecture, food, fashion..." she rambled on, getting carried away.

"Well, now that I'll be here in the States," Paul began, squeezing Lillie's hands. "My flat in Le Marais is available this summer if you like?" Paul said, encouraging her. "It would be no problem at all to arrange."

"If I like? Oh my gosh! Of course, I like. I would *love* that!" Chloe gushed.

"Well, you promised you'd be here to help with the tasting room, Chloe," Zach gently interjected.

"But this is a chance of a lifetime, Dad! Imagine how my portfolio would look after a summer in Paris?" She practically squealed in delight.

"You are much too young to do this on your own, Chloe."

Zach grew fatherly, and Kate could see Chloe begin to wilt.

"Oh, Zach, I'm sure she'd be fine, and after all, Paul and Lillie could connect her with their friends. She's practically twenty already," Kate said, trying to help.

"Kate, this is none of your business," Zach said quietly and firmly, and she felt as though he'd slapped her cheek. The joy of the wine and food immediately dissipated.

He turned to his daughter. "Chloe, we can talk about this another time." He regained his composure, then took another sip of wine.

Caroline eyed Kate and saw the hurt in her eyes. "Well, how about this beautiful winery? I think this is gorgeous, and I for one can't wait to see more of this town of Fredericksburg," she said, trying to lighten the mood.

"Yes!" Lillie brightened and squeezed Chloe's

arm. "How about we walk Main Street when we are done to look in the storefronts?"

"That sounds perfect. Especially after that flight today, I could use the opportunity to stretch my legs," Caroline said and took another sip of wine.

The conversation picked up again as Zach avoided Kate's eyes and she tried her best not to let his remark affect her. It was the first time he'd ever been unkind, and she hadn't been prepared for it. She began to question his character, remembering how her ex-husband could change from charmer to devil in an instant.

Zach wasn't David. She took a deep breath and let it out, turning her focus to the reason for the dinner and her sister's happiness.

Kate paid the bill, thanking the owners as they all made their way up the stone steps into the courtyard. The courtyard was emptying out as it was getting toward closing time. Caroline put her arm around Kate, and they made their way between the tables and spilled out onto the Main Street sidewalk.

A few blocks later, Kate pointed out the Winsome Winery tasting room storefront across the street. It was dark and empty inside. "Don't worry, it's going to be beautiful for your wedding day!" she promised her sister.

"It truly will be. Kate's done an amazing job," Zach said. He seemed to be trying to get her attention, but she resisted his gaze.

"I can't wait to see it!" Lillie beamed and hugged Paul closer.

Chloe and Zach walked together, and he put his arm around her and gave her a fatherly squeeze. "We'll talk," he whispered in her ear, and she grinned and squeezed him back.

The group walked down one side of the street and then the other, peering intently into the brightly lit storefront windows, until they made it back to the parking lot at Pontotoc.

Everyone hugged and kissed goodbye, and

then Lillie and Paul got into their rental. "Don't forget, breakfast tomorrow!" Kate called out right before they closed the door.

Chloe gave Kate a big hug and then took her dad's keys to get into his Range Rover. Caroline gave Zach a hug and looked at him sideways before getting into Kate's Durango.

After she shut the door, Kate and Zach were alone, and she felt awkward for the first time in a while.

"Kate. Listen, I'm sorry," he said, knowing as he looked into her dark eyes that he had hurt her.

"It's fine. Really. I mean, she's your daughter. I shouldn't have interfered. I just got carried away with everyone being together," Kate said.

"Well, yes, the responsibility to raise her is my job. But I should never have snapped at you like that." His voice softened as he came up and rested his hand on her cheek. She slowly raised her eyes to his.

"I guess I'm just not quite ready to let the

reins go with Chloe. She still seems like my little girl in so many ways. I know that this would be a great opportunity for her," he tried to explain.

Kate took a deep breath and let it out. "Yes. Totally. And I'm sorry for butting in. You know, I was on my own so young that I forget that it's different for other girls." She looked up at him. "And she's your girl." Kate wondered what sort of role she would play in Chloe's life now that she was older and close with her own mother.

He looked at her. "Forgive me?"

She smiled and brushed the stubble on his cheek with the palm of her hand. "Of course."

They kissed then, not the fun, playful way they had before. This time it was delicate and strong. They both knew that this was an important moment in their lives together, and they didn't take it lightly. It was the first time they had disagreed about something, and Kate was grateful that Zach was man enough to talk through it rather than brush it under the rug.

Pulling away, he brushed her cheek again. "I love you, Kate."

Without hesitating, she answered back, "I love you, too, Zach."

They hugged pulling their bodies close together before parting and getting into their vehicles to drive off.

"You OK, darlin'?" Caroline asked.

"Yes," Kate said. "I'm good."

Then she turned the key in the ignition, and they made their way down the driveway, turning left on Main Street to head back for the night.

⇒ Twenty-Eight ⇐

The next morning Kate woke up early, excited at the realization that her sister and closest friend were just yards away from her trailer. She quickly dressed, made herself a cup of coffee, and then texted them both: "The breakfast train leaves in 15 min!"

Caroline responded without haste. "Bring me French roast."

Lillie replied, "Sounds good. Want to swing by my room and see the dress??"

Kate's eyes grew wide over her coffee mug as she typed back: "YES!!!"

She quickly pressed another cup for Caroline and then scurried across the gravel driveway to pound on her friend's door. Caroline opened it up and was completely coiffed already. She had on pressed jeans, flats, and a high-collar, starched, white button-up shirt, with a long single strand of large silver balls hanging from her neck.

"Wow! You look Tex-Fabulous!" Kate laughed and handed her the mug.

"I must be prepared for anything and everything," Caroline said, then took a long luxurious sip of coffee, humming her approval.

"Come," Kate said, grabbing her arm and leading her down the porch.

"What on earth? I don't have my purse!" she called after her.

"I've got two words for you: wedding

dress," Kate said, and she heard Caroline pick up her pace.

"Oh, yes! This is the best part of any wedding!" She came alongside as they made their way to Lillie's room.

Kate knocked on the bright turquoise door twice before Lillie opened and smiled broadly at them both. "Good morning, you two!" They hugged each other and entered.

The room was bright and clean with a vintage feel. Taking up the center of the room was a king-size bed with a brown-leather headboard and a Southwest-patterned blanket draped playfully over the soft white bedspread. Crisp white walls accented the rich wood in the floor, and Kate and Caroline took seats in the retro leather and wooden chairs near the front window.

"Did Paul already leave for the airport?" Kate asked, looking around.

"Yes, which is why I thought this would be

a perfect time to show you my dress!" Lillie grew animated as she went into the bathroom and then emerged holding a hanger with a dress underneath a sheet of plastic.

She pulled the plastic up and revealed an off-white, crocheted-lace dress with a V-neck collar. Kate and Caroline looked at each other sideways.

"Just wait until you see it on!" Lillie said and headed back into the bathroom to put it on.

Caroline didn't need to say anything. Her eyes disapproved, and one corner of her mouth cringed up like she had just tasted something unsavory.

Kate widened her eyes and pleaded with her silently as they heard Lillie come back out.

They looked at her speechless. And not in a good way.

"Where did you get that, Lillie?" Kate ventured to ask.

"The thrift store in Port Angeles. I couldn't believe I found something that would fit and be suitable for the wedding." Lillie turned around as Kate and Caroline swallowed hard.

The dress was completely unflattering to Lillie, if that was even possible. The bodice was too short, the skirt too large and long, and the crocheted lace had holes in places. It was horrible.

"We could just pinch it up here and there to make it work," Lillie said as she looked at herself in the mirror. "I mean, it doesn't really matter. It's just one day?"

"Oh, HAIL NAWWWW," Caroline interjected, rolling her eyes. Kate snapped her head around with a stern look, "Car!"

"Naww, I'm sorry, but gurl, you cannot get married in that dress." Caroline shook her head emphatically.

Lillie's face began to crumple, and big tears filled her eyes. "It's the only thing I can afford right now," she began sniffing.

"Now, sis," Kate quickly got up and crossed the room to hug her sister, "maybe we can help with this?" She wiped a tear away from her dear sister's cheek.

Kate then looked back with narrowed eyes at Caroline. "In fact, I do believe that Caroline was looking for the perfect wedding gift for you."

Caroline put down her coffee mug and clapped her hands together. "Yes! Let's go dress shopping!"

Lillie looked at them both with big, sad eyes. "But the wedding is tomorrow, and don't you have to order dresses months in advance?"

Kate smiled as she remembered the store she saw in Bee Cave just last week when she was shopping for decor. Bestow Bridal.

"Hang on. Why don't you get out of that dress, and I'm going to make a phone call."

———

An hour later, the three were standing inside the most beautiful bridal boutique. Lillie's eyes were wide as she took in all the dresses on the racks and began gently thumbing through them. Caroline and Kate chatted with the staff and then returned to present Lillie a look book.

"OK, all these gowns are off the rack. They specialize in helping brides on a tight timeline find something they can purchase and wear right away." Caroline didn't add that the gowns were also extremely affordable, considering other alternatives.

"Lillie, here's some of their collection." Kate pointed to the pictures. "They have their gowns organized according to styles; Lovely Laces, Uniquely You, Boho Chic, Fabulously Fitted, Princess Bride, and Glitz & Glam."

Lillie looked through the pictures and immediately pointed out a dress in the Boho Chic category. Kate and Caroline nodded in agreement. "Yes, that's what we thought as well."

The woman took Lillie's measurements and then a few minutes later brought a rolling rack with five dresses that she wanted Lillie to try.

"OK, now we're having fun!" Caroline said,

as she accepted a glass of champagne from another store attendant and settled into an oversize couch facing a bank of mirrors outside the dressing room.

Kate giggled and joined her. "I can't wait to see these dresses!" They clinked glasses, and just then Lillie emerged from her dressing room.

Kate gasped and nearly choked on her bubbles. Lillie had been transformed within minutes. Her flowing sundress had been replaced by the most gorgeous gown.

Delicate transparent straps that lay perfectly on Lillie's shoulders attached to a bodice that plunged gently into a long V. A beautiful brocade of white flowers covered the nude mesh and made for a striking overlay that gathered together gently at her waist, before spilling out over her growing bump in a flowy tulle skirt that just barely touched the ground.

"Bravo!" Caroline applauded and Lillie turned around and looked at herself in the mirror. The back also had a V that gathered at the waist, and the sides of the bodice had a delicate opening where the front and back met the waistline, creating a sexy touch with her delicate skin peeking through the flowered overlay.

Lillie beamed as her black bobbed haircut framed her face and accentuated her lovely neck and the plunging lines of the bodice. The tulle crested softly over her growing bump and seemed like part of the design.

"Wow! Lillie, you look stunning!" Kate finally caught her breath. "How do you feel?"

"Like a princess!" She twirled around in glee. "It's so beautiful, but not nearly as heavy as I thought it would be. Paul would love this!" She giggled and continued twirling before adding, "And I think I could sit and play music in it as well. It's just light as a feather!"

Caroline smiled at Kate and then looked at the clerk. "That's it, then. We'll take it." There was no need to look at any other dress. It fit perfectly, and Lillie was blushing like the bride that she was becoming.

Caroline followed the clerk to the front to settle up, and Kate came around behind her sister as she preened in the mirror.

"You look exquisite, sis. Mom would be so proud of you." They locked eyes in the mirror, and then Lillie turned around to give her a hug.

"Thank you, sis." She pulled away and smiled. "I think she'd be pretty proud of you too."

Caroline returned and said, "Why don't you get out of that, and let's grab something to eat."

"I really can't thank you enough, Caroline! This is the best gift ever!" Lillie hugged Caroline, who just nodded, smiling as tears touched her eyes.

"It's the least I can do for family." They held eyes for a moment before Lillie turned around and disappeared into the dressing room.

Kate held out her glass of champagne,

turning to her friend. "Well done, Car." They clinked glasses.

"Ah, you know I couldn't let that sweet girl get married in anything less than perfect. Something old, something new!" She winked, and they downed the last of the champagne as they set their glasses down. Lillie emerged, and the three of them made their way to the front of the store while the clerks boxed up the dress.

"Brunch?" Kate asked, wrapping one arm around Caroline and the other around Lillie, and they headed out together.

———

THE GIRLS MADE IT back to the motor lodge later that afternoon, and Caroline went to her cabin to take a nap. Lillie stashed her new dress for safe keeping with Kate, and then headed back to her room to meet Paul's parents.

Kate shook her head; it had been such a fun day. Looking at all those dresses was truly thrilling. The best part was seeing her little sister find the perfect dress for her, the very first one she tried. It was unbelievable, except Kate believed. She knew that once things started clicking, it all just flowed. She laughed thinking about the dress that Lillie was planning to wear, and then she imagined the look on Paul's face tomorrow when he sees his bride walk toward him under the twinkling lights. She flashed back to Lillie's question about whether she would ever get married again. Kate wasn't sure of that answer but felt like she was closer to at least being open to the possibility.

Her phone buzzed with a message from Zach. "Navajo Grill at 7 pm, right? XX"

She smiled and texted back with a thumb emoji and a kiss.

The clock in her trailer said four. She had enough time for a nap too. All that dress shopping, brunch, and driving had worn her out. Although Kate was happy to have Lillie and Caroline close, she wasn't used to the barrage

of social interaction. A nap would be the perfect reset.

She drew down the blackout curtains in her
trailer and set her alarm for five.

⇒ Twenty-Nine ⇐

Kate woke to the sound of her alarm, momentarily disoriented in the dark space. She had slept so deeply she'd forgotten where she was. After turning on her bedside reading light, she shut off her alarm and then stretched before heading for the shower.

An hour later, Kate was awake, dressed, and ready for dinner. Caroline had texted that she had decided to squeeze in a tasting, so she'd be meeting them at the restaurant. Lillie and Paul were driving his parents, so that left Kate alone in her Durango heading to the restaurant.

Twenty minutes later, she saw the building that seemed almost like a house tucked discreetly away. She pulled off Main Street and circled around to the back to find a parking spot. The limestone walkway was lit by soft yellow lights, and Kate passed through the courtyard to open one of the French doors to where the hostess stand was located.

Kate saw Caroline, Lillie, and Paul already inside, and waved as she approached their table. Next to Paul, his parents politely rose from their seats, and Kate came around to introduce herself. His mother, Martine, gave her a warm hug. Although quite a bit shorter than Kate, she had a commanding presence. His father, Didier, had an endearing face and a strong handshake. Soon after, Zach arrived, and introductions were made all around.

Zach settled into a seat beside Kate and

gently patted her leg underneath the table. She smiled and, turning to Mr. and Mrs. Comtois, asked, "How was your trip in?"

"Ah, superbe!" Martine spoke as the waiter made it around the table, pouring flat and sparkling water.

"Wonderful. Have you been to Texas before?" Kate asked, as she took a sip of water and Zach perused the wine list.

"*Non.* But we hear that this state is the same size as our entire country!" Didier laughed with his belly, which made everyone laugh with him.

"Texas is its own country!" Caroline interjected, joining in the laughter.

Kate nodded in agreement. "Tell me, you are from Burgundy?"

"*Oui.* Our ancestors are actually from the *Franche-Compté* region, which is now merged with Bourgogne," Martine stated with her lips pursed.

Paul gently injected, "But it is easier to just

say Bourgogne, or Burgundy, as people outside of France do not know the difference. *C'est la même chose!*"

They all chuckled, and Zach ordered a few bottles of wine before turning back into the conversation. "An impressive region of wine making, isn't it?"

"The finest!" Didier said. "We enjoy the best fruits of the region: beef, wine, and of course, Dijon mustard!"

"As do we." Zach smiled warmly, then winked. "At least we can import the Dijon mustard."

The two men nodded in agreement and before long the wine was flowing. Steak frites, stuffed quails, and braised short rib was ordered for the table, while everyone sat back and enjoyed learning a bit about each other and the differences and similarities in their cultures.

Before long, Zach and Didier began talking about growing grapes and what it was like to produce in France compared to Texas.

"We are blessed with weather, altitude, and terrain," Didier said.

"Here, it's a bit more difficult. In fact, it's a lot more difficult to cultivate fruit so that it will produce the finest wines. Between the heat, frosts, hail, and insects, we are constantly on guard. Thankfully the community is very close, and we gain a lot of knowledge by sharing tips and resources with each other," Zach said.

"Roses?" Martine stated.

"I beg your pardon?" Zach asked, feeling as though he had missed something in the conversation.

"Have you planted your roses?" Martine asked and nudged Didier.

Zach looked at Didier to explain.

"In our region, one of the first ways we know if pests are damaging our crops is with rosebushes. We plant them at the end post of each row and monitor their health closely." He nodded to Zach. "They not only look beautiful but are quick to show the first signs of insect or other damage, so that we can address the vines accordingly."

"Wow, that's interesting! I don't think that's been done here, although that could be due to the extreme heat we have in summer." He raised his glass to Didier. "What a fantastic idea, though!"

"I love that idea! Y'all need to do that," Caroline agreed and took another sip of her wine.

Kate smiled, basking in the easy exchange at the table. She loved learning more about winemaking in France. There was so much for her yet to learn just in Texas, let alone the centuries of tips and tricks that were passed down in France. It made her want to take a trip abroad again, this time to focus solely on wine making and growing.

The food arrived, and they continued to get acquainted between bites.

"This food is all locally sourced, which I find

really enhances the experience when you pair it with Texas wines," Zach explained as they dished out servings onto their plates. "Unfortunately, they do not offer Texas wines on the menu. However, tomorrow our food and wine pairing from the Ab Astris winery will give you a true taste of what we have to offer here in the Hill Country."

"Ah, bien sûr!" Didier said. "Of course! Everything that comes from the land, above and below, must remain together. They work in harmony with the sun, wind, rain, and soil. You cannot transplant it from elsewhere."

Zach nodded. "I think I understand your meaning. And I agree. The fact that everything grown in a certain region will have the same elements and that just enhances the authenticity of the flavors."

"Precisely. *C'est tout!*" Didier exclaimed.

Kate caught Zach's eyes, and they both had a moment of agreement, knowing that the decision they had made to focus on making 100 percent Texas wine was absolutely the right one.

"We are so thrilled that our son is marrying such a beautiful, talented young woman!" Martine said, changing the subject, as Lillie blushed in the warm glow of the dining room.

"Our son has not always found it easy to date," Didier said as Paul rolled his eyes.

"Papa, we do not need to share this much," he pleaded.

"Well, it is true, *non*?" He then looked at Zach and Kate conspiratorially. "He has always been good at technical things—playing guitar and software. But he was never good at talking with the females."

"*Papa, s'il vous plaît...*" Paul blushed as everyone around the table chuckled.

"Neither was Lillie!" Kate said, sharing a bit more about her sister, much to her chagrin. "She was always a wonderful dreamer and talented at whatever she did. But she was also terrible at dating."

"Sis!" Lillie implored.

They all laughed, and Didier said, "Then, it's *bon chance*, good luck, that they found each other!"

They all agreed and raised their glasses to toast the blushing and beautiful couple as they looked into each other's eyes and sweetly kissed.

"A perfect couple," Caroline said and winked at Kate.

Hands clapped, and cheers went around the table.

Kate was so pleased at how lovely Paul and his family were. It was a welcome surprise, and she felt like not only were they bringing Lillie into their family, but they were accepting Kate as well.

It was better than anything Kate could have imagined herself. She was full of good food, delicious wine, and wonderful company: her new family. It wasn't what she expected, but perhaps it was even better.

———

MUCH TOO SOON, THE evening ended, and they said their goodbyes as Lillie drove Paul and his parents back to the motor lodge. Caroline hugged them and headed back to call Rob and the kids. Finally, Zach walked Kate towards the parking lot.

"Kate, hang on a minute. Do you mind having a nightcap?" he asked her, holding out his hand.

She looked at her watch; it was only eight-thirty. "Sure." She took Zach's hand, and he led her back into the now empty courtyard and over to a dimly lit table in the corner.

The bartender came around to take their order and placed a single candle in the middle of the table. The flame instantly brightened and softened their features, and it seemed as though they were alone together for the first time in weeks.

Zach reached for her hand over the table and then began to softly caress the tops of her fingers. "Kate, I feel like we haven't had much time together, and part of that is my fault, with all the wine business and craziness," he began to explain.

"No, it's me too. All this wedding stuff, and having everyone here, has been pretty overwhelming," she said.

"I hope you don't think I'm neglecting you." He looked into her eyes. "I find it hard to balance the business, Chloe, and a new relationship."

"I think you are doing an excellent job. Really." She squeezed his hand. "I honestly think we've been doing a good job of communicating in spite of all the obstacles," she said as the waiter returned and placed two glasses of Merlot in front of them.

"Even with the incident the other night?" he asked as he gently swirled his wine around in the glass.

"Yes," she answered honestly. "We aren't going to be perfect, Zach. We are going to have our issues, and I think we did a great job of handling it."

She reached her glass over to touch the rim of his.

"You are very gracious, but I would never want to do anything to hurt you," he said and cleared his throat. "I just want you to know I don't take it lightly."

"I believe you," she said. "I trust you."

"I hope you do," he said, and pulled his phone out of his jacket pocket. "I want to show you something."

Kate looked at him, curious as she peered at the lit-up screen he slid in front of her. She saw it was a Zillow app with a listing of a house. Kate's gut knotted a bit as she wondered where this was leading.

"Don't worry, I heard what you said the other night at dinner. I do need to move closer to the

tasting room, and I found this amazing property." He said and then flicked the photos until
she saw a detached garage with a large cement
pad next to it. "Look! It already has full hookups
for an RV." He peered at her, his eyes dancing.

"You're kidding!" She looked at it, and the
reality began to hit her.

"You can hitch up and stay for however long
or short you want. You'll have your own space
and be able to enjoy your Airstream, but we can
also spend more time together too." He grinned
at her. "A perfect compromise."

Kate started laughing, and then it grew into
the biggest belly laugh until tears were falling
down her cheeks. He looked questioningly at
her, wondering if he'd said something wrong.

Finally, she wiped her cheeks and patted him
on the shoulder. "You did good." She laughed
again softer, "Zach Winsome, you are the most
amazing man. To think that you would get a
property with an RV pad solely so that I would

be comfortable—it's something I would never dream of myself." She grabbed him and pulled close to kiss him softy and warmly on the lips. Salty and sweet.

They pulled away. "I'm so relieved," he said. "I didn't know whether you would be OK with it or not."

"It's really perfect, Zach. Truly." Kate smiled at him, and they kissed again.

Thirty

The next day emerged bright and full of hope. Kate stretched in bed, grateful that she had been able to get some deep sleep, in spite of all the excitement. She felt strangely refreshed.

"Lillie's day!" she sang and opened all the blinds as the birds chirped and flitted about in the pecan and oak trees that dotted the property.

After firing up her hot water for coffee, she put on some jazz music and hummed to herself as she pulled out her wedding-day checklist.

She had rented an Airbnb downtown just a

block from the winery for the bridal party to get dressed. The groom's party would take over the tasting room.

The wedding was scheduled for five, with the reception and dinner to follow. Zach was in charge of picking up the cases of wine from storage, and the flat and sparkling water would be delivered to the tasting room.

Kate had already decorated the patio of the tasting room, the only thing left was to pick up the flower arrangements today at noon. She'd arrange the centerpieces at all the tables and then meet Lillie, Caroline, and Chloe at the rental to get ready and have girls' time before the festivities. She had a case of champagne in her Durango and had ordered a charcuterie board from Fredericksboards to be delivered to the rental at two-thirty.

She finished sipping her coffee, then jumped into the shower. Ella crooned as she finished up and then she dressed quickly in jeans and a tank top before drying her hair. She looked at the clock—it was already eleven!

Her phone buzzed and she grabbed it to see a message from Zach. "Good morning! Everything is set up at the tasting room and just waiting for the caterers to arrive. Hope you slept well? XX"

She grinned and texted back: "I tossed and turned a bit, but finally got to sleep. I'm just so excited for Lillie's day! I'm heading out to get the flowers. See you soon! Xo"

She then texted Caroline the address of the rental with a message: "See you at one! Don't forget to bring those bottles I gave you to chill!"

Finally a message to Lillie: "Good morning, beautiful bride to be!! See you at one! Do you need anything?"

A few bubbles as Lillie replied: "I'm good! Can't believe this is happening! See you soon!"

Another bubble appeared from Caroline: "Yes'm! xoxo"

Kate turned off her phone and started

packing her go bag with makeup, curling irons, hair products, heels, and jewelry. She then grabbed her phone charger off the counter, shoved it into her clutch purse, and scanned the Airstream for any other items she may have forgotten. She loaded everything, including her dress, into the Durango, then jumped in and started it up to head into town.

———

JUST UP THE WAY from the motor lodge, she reached Wildseed Farms, one of the largest wildflower farms near Fredericksburg. She had chosen to prepurchase enough bluebonnets for the table centerpieces and to make Lillie a bridal bouquet. While she could have pulled off the road and just cut these flowers herself, she felt a little weird about that. It was better to support a local farm and leave the landscape naturally wild.

Kate had read about the origin of the blue-bonnet: Lady Bird Johnson encouraged Texans to plant and cultivate wildflowers as part of the Texas Highway Beautification Act of 1965. Soon, the hills were vibrant with the colors of bluebonnets and black-eyed Susans. Kate felt it very strange to remove what thousands of tourists came every year to use as a backdrop for family photos or self-portraits showing their Texas pride.

She secured the happy flowers in her Durango and then continued on to the Flower Pail to pick up her pre-ordered bulk white and green roses. Once she got everything together, she headed straight downtown to the tasting room and began bringing everything inside.

Zach was behind the bar counter, and he came around to help her unload the flowers and carry them to the back patio.

"Can you please grab the case of champagne and put that in the fridge for us?" Kate asked as she made her way out for the last load of flowers.

"You bet." He grabbed the case and then

placed it on top of the bar. Then turned quickly around to kiss her as she passed by. She giggled, thinking about how maybe she would have her cake and eat it too.

The idea that she could still have her own space and embrace RV life, while also taking their relationship to the next stage, made Kate giddy. It gave her a renewed sense of independence and security at the same time.

She grabbed her pruning shears and set them to the side as she opened up the boxes of flowers and spread out the beautiful colors. She began building small bunches, bringing a few roses together with the bluebonnets adding a vivid contrast, and then she cut the stems and placed them in the Mason jars that were already wrapped with ribbon in the center of each table.

"Here, let me help," Zach said, as he picked up the vases and took them two by two into the tasting room to fill them halfway with water and return them in time for Kate to plunge the flowers in the center and arrange the foliage just right.

She hummed while she worked and after a while stood back and took in the room. It was better than she imagined. The white and soft green of the roses set off the brilliance of the bluebonnets. The arrangements were simple and rustic but classic. She knew that once they lit the votives and the rest of the lights, everything would create the perfect romantic setting.

She had set aside some of the best flowers for last. She bunched them together by the fistful and then tied a silk ribbon around the stems and pinned them into place. The bridal bouquet.

"Kate, you are really good at this," Zach said as he came up behind her and put his arm around her waist.

"Thank you. I have to say, I think I may have outdone myself." She grinned and then leaned into him while still taking in the whole scene.

"I think that's it. I just need to get rid of all

this," she said, motioning to the debris from the flower cuttings and boxes, "and then head to the bridal suite to get ready."

"I've got this," Zach said. "You go on. The caterers just arrived, and they are setting up in the tasting room. I'll manage all this and text you if anything comes up."

"Thanks, handsome." She grinned, giving him a quick peck on the cheek and lingering for a moment before turning on her heels.

"Chloe should be there soon!" he called out to her, and she waved back with the bridal bouquet overhead before scurrying out the door.

She then reparked her Durango up the block and around the corner where the Airbnb was located. She saw that Caroline's rental car was already there.

"Helloooo!" she sang out as she opened the front door and was greeted with cheers.

Caroline came up and gave her a big smooch on the cheeks. "It's about time you got here! I just opened that viognier. Let's get this pre-brid-al party started!"

Lillie followed and gave her a big squeeze before asking, "Where's Chloe?"

Just then, a rap on the door gave them that answer. Lillie bounded over and opened up to see her new friend arrive. They helped each other unload their cars with all the bags and dresses and paraphernalia. The room was soon full with sounds of joy and merriment, and Kate relished the sounds. Although she had done quite a bit of planning, it was a fairly casual affair, and she was just happy to finally have checked off all her lists and be able to focus on getting gussied up as well.

Lillie and Chloe settled in front of the gor-geous antique vanity with a huge mirror and took turns helping each other with their hair. "I can't wait to see your dress!!" Kate heard Chloe tell Lillie as they bantered back and forth.

"Everything all set at the winery?" Caroline

asked as she and Kate took chairs across the room and sipped their wine.

"It is," Kate beamed. "I absolutely love the flower arrangements, and once the lights are on, it will be truly spectacular."

Kate called to Lillie over her shoulder, "Zach said he was able to borrow that PA and mics, so all you and Paul have to do is plug and play."

"Wonderful! Paul's in charge of the instruments, but I made sure everything was packed in the car before Caroline and I came." Lillie grinned and continued her lively conversation with Chloe.

"And what are *you* wearing?" Kate pointed her glass at Caroline and watched her raise an eyebrow.

"Oh, just a little number that I call 'Fabulous.'" She giggled as she tipped her glass.

Another rap at the door, and Kate opened to see their charcuterie from Fredericksboards. She signed the receipt, added a generous tip, then brought the board in to place it on the desk where everyone quickly gathered.

"Oh, this is adorable!" Caroline gushed as she grabbed a cucumber slice.

The bamboo tray held an assortment of meats, cheeses, fresh and dried fruits, nuts, crackers, olives, and some chocolates. A perfect amount for the four of them to enjoy.

"This is perfect, sis! I needed something in my belly, but there's no way I could eat much before the ceremony," Lillie said as she picked at the tray.

Caroline topped off Kate's glass of wine, and then they settled back in to watch Lillie get ready.

Her straight black hair naturally curved under her chin, so there wasn't much to perfect there. Chloe was laying out all her makeup options when Lillie said, "Who wants to see the wedding ring?"

Caroline gave Kate a wink, and then they

all came over to the vanity where Lillie pulled out of a pouch a delicate platinum setting with scrollwork and a small yellow diamond in the center.

"Lillie! Where did Paul find this? It's absolutely gorgeous," Kate said as she leaned in to get a better look.

"Oh, this has to be antique. Did he get it from his parents?" Caroline asked her.

"*Oui!*" she giggled. "It's over one hundred years old, his grandmother's ring, and they gave it to us!"

"Oh, that is just precious. It looks perfect on you," Kate said as Chloe nudged her aside.

"Hold your hand out. I want to get a few pictures." She focused her camera lens manually and snapped a few pictures at different angles. She looked at the viewfinder. "Perfect."

Lillie dug through her purse and pulled out a handsome platinum band, then handed both rings to Kate. "Can you keep these safe until the ceremony?"

"Absolutely," Kate said as she tucked them back into their pouch and placed them into her silk clutch.

The next couple of hours were filled with laughter, curling irons, makeup, and excitement until finally it was time for everyone to get into their dresses.

Kate slid on her silk gown, and everyone agreed that it was the perfect dress for her. The colors gave her skin a glow, and the halter top made her neck seem even longer. She had chosen to curl her hair for volume and then pin it up in a French twist in the back, with just a few strands framing her face.

Caroline was next, and she chose a gorgeous black boatneck dress that was covered in delicate, shiny-black beadwork. It was simple and elegant, and she accented it perfectly with a thick solid-gold chain with a beautiful old medallion hanging from the center.

Chloe revealed her selection, which was a very sweet spaghetti-strapped dark-purple chiffon dress with a princess waist and a skirt that came just down to her knees. She had a matching delicate crystal necklace and earrings that were offset by a beautiful rhinestone flower hairpin that held her bangs back.

Finally, it was time for the bride.

Lillie walked into the room looking even more stunning than she had when she first tried the dress on, if that was even possible. Her skin was radiant, and the dress fit her perfectly. Everyone gasped and applauded in agreement.

Chloe grabbed her camera and immediately went to work, getting as many shots as possible from different angles and in different positions.

She finally lowered her camera and said, "You are the most beautiful bride I've ever seen." Lillie teared up and gave her a hug.

"Don't mess up her makeup!" Caroline called out as the two girls pulled away and giggled.

It was now four-thirty. A half hour to the ceremony.

"OK, I'm going to head over there and text you, Caroline, when everyone is in their seats and you can walk over," Kate said as she grabbed her lipstick and mints from her bag and stuffed them into the clutch, double-checking that the pouch with the rings was still there.

"Text me if you need anything, and I'll see you soon!" Kate said as she walked towards the door. "Oh! Your bouquet!" Kate exclaimed as she remembered the bridal bouquet was still in the backseat of her SUV. She quickly ran out to get it and returned presenting it to Lillie.

"Sis, these are gorgeous!" Lillie's eyes took in every detail of the delicate flowers as Chloe began taking shots.

"I think we have everything that we are supposed to have for a wedding, right?" Kate asked.

"Something old..." Chloe said and then added, "the antique ring!"

"Something new..." Lillie said and then grinned at Caroline, "my dress!"

"Something borrowed..." Kate couldn't think of anything she had to lend to her sister.

"I have it!" Chloe quickly pulled the rhinestone-flower pin out of her hair and gently placed it in Lillie's dark locks. It was the perfect finishing touch.

"Something blue," Caroline said, and they all said together, "Bluebonnets!" As Lillie held up her bouquet.

Kate basked in the glow of their laughter, taking a mental snapshot of this special moment. It had all come together just as she suspected it would. She then grabbed her clutch and hurried out the door to head to the tasting room.

⇉Thirty-One⇇

Kate looked out onto the patio and saw that everyone was in position. Dennis was standing underneath the lit-up oak, with the paper cutout stars floating gracefully in the light breeze. Paul was standing to the left of Dennis wearing a gorgeous dark suit with an off-white silk tie. Paul's parents were seated in front, with Caroline and Chloe on the other side of the aisle.

It was time.

The music changed and the song by Sara

Bareilles that Lillie and Paul had chosen for the procession began playing.

From the doorway, Lillie emerged holding Kate's arm. Everyone turned in their seats, and the electricity was palpable as Paul's eyes grew wide, taking in the picture of Lillie in the most perfect gown, making her way slowly towards him.

Tell the world that we finally got it all right
I choose you
I will become yours and you will become mine
I choose you

Kate walked Lillie to the front and then stepped to the side as she took her place across from Zach.

The music faded out as Lillie and Paul stood across from each other, a foot apart, staring lovingly into each other's eyes in anticipation.

"We have come together this evening to join these two in holy matrimony," Dennis began, and Kate and Zach looked into each other's eyes and held for a long moment. "In this world, it is easy to be cynical or to believe that love can't really happen. This is precisely why we come together in front of our dear friends and family at special moments like these. To bear witness to the miracle and to acknowledge that true, everlasting love does exist."

Kate looked out at her dear friend Caroline and saw that she was already crying.

When it came time for the rings, Zach passed Paul the ring for Lillie first.

"With this ring, I thee wed and promise to honor and cherish you until death," Paul said and gently placed the ring on Lillie's shaking finger.

Kate handed Paul's band to Lillie.

"With this ring, I thee wed and promise to honor and cherish you until death," she said as she slid his band onto his ring finger.

"With the power vested in me by this great state of Texas, and before God, I now pronounce you man and wife." Dennis raised his arms. "You may kiss!"

Lillie and Paul came together and kissed, then pulled back, eyes locked in mutual love, with happy tears flowing as they turned to their friends and family, held hands, and raised them up triumphantly to cheers and applause.

———

ZACH TOOK KATE'S HAND as everyone made their way inside to the tasting room. The catering staff had set the tables together so there was one long length that flanked the expanse of the bar. Even though the party was only twelve in total, Kate had assigned seats with tent name cards, and everyone talked and greeted one another as they found their seats. Each place setting had four empty glasses in front for each of the upcoming courses. There were beautiful crystal vases in the center of the table filled with flat water, and the staff came around to fill sparkling water for those who preferred.

The bride and groom stayed behind to take photos on the patio with Chloe before making their entrance inside.

Everyone stood and applauded as Lillie came in beside Paul, their cheeks aglow with the warmth of their new vows and commitment to each other.

Once they were seated, the catering staff began pouring wine into glasses as the first course was served.

Zach stood. "We are pleased to be serving you four courses lovingly prepared by The Liquid Culture, with wine pairings from Ab Astris Winery." Sighs of delight could be heard around the room. "All of the food is locally sourced; the produce and vegetables from Hat & Heart, the meat from ROAM Ranch, and the fruit from Jenschke Orchards. Please enjoy!"

They *oohed* and *awed* as the plates appeared before them. Beautifully lined asparagus tips lay on top of sourdough toast, drizzled delicately

with an aioli and topped with watermelon rad-
ishes and shavings of salt-cured egg yolk.

"This looks fabulous, darlin'!" Caroline said
as she began to cut into her toast.

Kate pointed to the bread. "The chef makes
that sourdough himself from Barton Springs
Mill flour out of Dripping Springs. You can't
get more local than that!"

They each took a bite, enjoying all the
flavors before washing them down with the
wine pairing, a 2020 Estate Petillant Naturel.
"This delightful sparkling wine is made from
Clairette Blanche grapes grown on the estate
at Ab Astris," Zach said as he raised his glass
to the table.

The wine was dry, with a slight residue of
sugar that balanced the acidity nicely and paired
perfectly with the course. Kate heard murmurs
of approval at the end of the table .

Next, the staff came around to replace their
plates with the next course and to remove their

first glass and pour wine into their second. "For the next course, we introduce a unique take on the Potato Pave." The crispy squares of pressed potato had been fried to a perfect crisp and placed on a bed of thick chicken-stock roux containing bright green peas and baby rainbow carrots. "We have chosen to pair this selection with the 2017 Cabernet Sauvignon. Traditionally, a cab would be a bit too heavy for this pairing, but you'll find that the cabs in Texas are much lighter than their Napa Valley counterparts, due to their higher acidity levels. Which makes for a delightful taste to compliment the rich layers of potato, cream, and butter."

They all began slicing down the layers to the thick sauce and then taking each bite. Kate's eyes rolled back. "I am such a sucker for potatoes, cream, and butter anything...this is so divine. Crispy and savory!" She took a sip of her Cabernet and nodded. "And a perfect pairing with the wine. I would have thought maybe white, but this works so well." Zach took a sip as he hummed in agreement.

Once the table finished, the next course was presented. "You will see on your plates sustainable and regeneratively grown venison rib chops," Zach explained. "They are covered with a pesto made of English peas with mint. A perfect combination for spring here in the Hill Country." Everyone enjoyed the presentation, and Chloe snapped a few pictures. "We have paired this course with the 2018 Tempranillo. Need we say more?" They all laughed and dug into this next course.

It was just enough meat on the bone to satisfy, but not too much to overfill. Wine glasses tipped all around the table as they sipped the Tempranillo and delighted in the classic cherry and black-pepper finish. Caroline wiped the sides of her mouth with her cloth napkin. "I declare this is absolutely the perfect pairing menu so far!"

"Well, hope you have room for one more: the dessert course!" Kate winked at her friend as the rest of the table finished up.

"Finally, we bring you to our last course. Lillie and Paul both said they loved strawberries, and we just happen to have the most delicious ones grown in a local greenhouse," Zach said as the staff brought the last plating and poured the final glass of wine.

"We have an almond olive oil cake topped with fresh strawberries and Chantilly cream," he said as sounds of overwhelming approval rose around the table. "We are pairing this with the 2020 Stello, a blend of Roussanne, Clairette Blanche, Picpoul Blanc, and Marsanne. A delightful, fruit-forward white."

They lowered their forks into the cream, strawberries, and luscious cake. Conversation turned into *mmm*s as they savored each bite and then sipped the delightful wine.

"When you are finished, please feel free to

adjourn to the patio as Lillie and Paul will have their first dance and then will perform some of their beautiful music for us. We also will be serving champagne at the bar, compliments of the groom's family!" Kate motioned to the Comtois. "Thank you, Martine and Didier!" She raised her glass to them as everyone nodded and a few clapped their hands in gratitude.

As the staff began picking up plates, Kate helped Zach behind the bar, popping open bottles of champagne and pouring glasses for everyone. There was much laughter and cheers shared by all. Everyone marveled at how stunning Lillie looked in her gown, and Paul stayed close to her side as the happy couple basked in the glow of their love and the love of everyone in the room.

"To Lillie and Paul." Zach took two glasses and held one out to Kate.

"To Lillie and Paul," she echoed back as she took the glass.

They clinked and then sipped, the bubbles tingling their throats and warming their bellies. The guests took a chance to tour the tasting room and comment on how beautiful it looked, asking questions about the opening.

"Just a month away!" Zach said as his smile grew and he looked at Kate with pride.

As the crowd moved back out to the patio, Kate and Zach stepped from behind the bar and headed out to the small area they had cleared for dancing.

Everyone stood at the periphery as they watched Lillie and Paul take their first dance as husband and wife. The newlyweds laughed and kissed gently as they swayed back and forth in perfect rhythm. Zach put his arm around Kate's waist, and she pictured what it would be like if this were their first dance.

Throughout the whole ceremony, in the back of Kate's mind, thoughts of her and Zach's relationship were not far behind. In fact, something about the way Dennis talked about everlasting love reassured Kate in a way. The fears of her past experiences seemed to recede as she began to consider that perhaps someday she would be married again. Instead, she felt the presence of this man next to her, the man she had prayed for relentlessly. She watched him as his face openly displayed his love for Lillie and Paul's union. She watched Chloe move expertly in and out of the crowd capturing candid shots.

She knew that there was no one else she would rather be with right now. Or ever.

"Do you remember how to dance?" she teased as she set down her champagne flute.

"Oh, I may even have some new moves." He grinned and took her right hand to lead her out to the dance floor where they joined a few other couples.

He pulled her close, and Kate felt the strength of his arms and his chest against hers. Her mind and body instantly shivered in delight as they began to sway slowly back and forth in the small space.

His left hand was holding her right, with his other hand at her waist, guiding her. Her left arm was draped around his neck, and she let her fingertips massage the base of his neck where his hair grew a little longer. He snuggled his face into the side of her neck, kissing it sweetly and then resting his cheek to hers as he glided her around in small circles.

The song finished and they pulled apart. "Is it time to pour more champagne?"

He let both of his arms glide down hers until he held her hands, "Shall we?" Zach took her hand, and they made their way back into the tasting room. They chose bottles and then made their way around the room to top off the guests' glasses.

The pure notes from Lillie's fiddle skimmed the air outside on the patio. Paul plucked his guitar strings as she wove her melody in between his notes, making a beautiful tapestry of sound. Her soft voice lilted over their heads and seemed to float, as though coming from another place or time. At the chorus, Paul joined her, harmonizing low so their intertwined voices created one magnified note.

"Wow, they are so perfect together!" Kate said out loud as she watched them, mesmerized.

"A match made from heaven for sure." Caroline nodded to her friend, equally enchanted, before sauntering off to refill her glass.

Chloe took a break from taking pictures of the couple and their guests and set her camera on the metal table to plop down on one of the chairs.

"Are you getting good shots?" Kate asked, already knowing that answer.

"The lighting is perfect. The couple is perfect. What more could I ask for?" She laughed in satisfaction.

Zach pulled up a chair close to Kate, and

they all basked in the afterglow of an amazing wedding party. The ceremony was perfect. The dinner pairing with Ab Astris wines was a hit. Zach and Kate were more than proud to see the approval on the faces of the Comtoises as they delighted with each bite.

"So, Chloe. I meant to talk to you earlier," Zach said leaned over the table. "Maybe it's a good idea for you get away for the summer...to Paris," he began.

"What? Dad! Really?" Her face lit up with hope.

Zach chuckled, unable to keep a straight face. "Yes. If Paul's flat is available, you can go spend the summer in the Marais." He had hardly finished the sentence before she had flung her arms around his head, squealing with delight.

"Thank you, Dad! Thank you!" she exclaimed.

"But there will be some ground rules, which

we'll go over tomorrow." He unconvincingly tried to sound firm. "And, maybe Kate and I can make a trip to visit as well?" He eyed Kate as her smile grew wide.

"Yes, of course! This will be so amazing! It's totally about my photography," Chloe said earnestly.

"Well, and maybe about the cheese and the meat and the architecture and the music..." Kate trailed off and laughed with Chloe. "You are going to have a fabulous time, Chloe! I'll definitely want to see those shots."

Chloe hugged her, then grabbed her camera and danced off, inspired to take more shots of the bride and groom.

Kate chuckled. "So, you changed your mind?"

"Well, it's truly a once in a lifetime opportunity. And she is a big girl. I know that I can trust her." He reached over to caress Kate's forearm. "Thank you for the reminder that we all need to grow and evolve."

"Anytime." She locked eyes with him as the music swelled.

"Ok, get a room, you two!" Caroline laughed, as she danced by.

Dennis ambled over. "Howdy!"

They both got up and hugged him. "It was a wonderful service, Dennis!" Kate gushed, and Zach patted his back in agreement.

"Oh, it's easy to come up with the right words when you're inspired. Those two are very sweet, and I wish them a very long, happy life together."

They all clinked their glasses to that toast.

"So, Kate, will you be joining us for harvest this year?" Dennis asked.

"I can't wait! After seeing the vines budding a few weeks ago, I can't wait to be part of the entire process," she said. "Do we know when that will be?"

"Well, it depends on the varietal and the weather. Usually, it's early to late August, but the growers and Leah will make the call. It's a very last-minute hustle to get all hands on deck," Dennis explained. "We want them to be just ripe enough, but then that gives us a short window to get all the grapes off the vines before they're overripe."

Kate nodded in excitement. "I will be ready."

Zach chimed in, "We all will!"

The music ended, and Kate watched Lillie and Paul slowly making their way around the tables to thank the guests for coming. They came around to their table, and Lillie hugged Dennis and thanked him again for the beautiful words. Paul hugged him and kissed both his cheeks, as well, which made him slightly uncomfortable and made Kate and Lillie giggle.

"Sis, the music you and Paul make is absolutely beautiful. I wish you weren't going back to Port Angeles. That you could play here all the time!" She squeezed her sister.

Lillie looked at Paul and then back at Kate

and Zach. "Well, if you are looking for a house band...we have been thinking that maybe we should relocate here to the Hill Country."

"Really?" Kate's eyes lit up.

"Yes, there is a huge tech boom in Austin right now, and Paul works remotely as it is. And besides, we'd rather be close to you and the winery," Lillie said. "It's been great being back to the Northwest to revisit and get some things settled, but I don't want to be that far away from you...especially when the baby comes."

Kate and Lillie hugged, and Kate felt everything coming together. She had been worried about Lillie leaving again, and having her decide to move to Texas instead was icing on the cake.

She looked at Dennis and Zach for any sign of objection. Dennis replied, "As far as I'm concerned, you are hired." Zach nodded emphatically in agreement. "Absolutely, yes!"

"Perfect!" Lillie said, looking up at Paul. "We

should probably make our rounds." They walked off together as Kate was stunned speechless.

"Wow. Who'd have thought everything would work out so well?" Zach spoke her inner thoughts out loud as she nodded in agreement.

Paul's parents came over and sat down in the empty seats.

"We just want to thank you again for this lovely evening," Martine said, her skin looking even more beautiful in the soft glow of the lights.

"The food and wine pairings were *trés magnifique*!" Didier exclaimed. "I never thought I would have that kind of culinary experience here in Texas."

"Ah, that is music to my ears. We have so much more to offer here than just cowboys and cattle." Zach grinned.

"I'm so glad you both enjoyed it, and your son is just precious. I'm thrilled that he is part of the family now," Kate said.

"As are you!" Didier said.

"*Oui!* You must come to Bourgogne and visit our vineyards," Martine insisted. "You can stay with us, and we will share with you the cuisine and wine that our region is famous for."

Kate and Zach shrugged to each other, "We'd love to!"

"*C'est parfait,*" Martine said.

"Of course, we will be in touch as we get closer to the due date too. I'll be sure Paul gives you all of our contact information, and we'll plan to come back again to visit after the birth," Didier stated.

"That sounds perfect. They are going to make wonderful parents," Kate said.

"We will all help!" Martine said, and they all toasted their glasses together.

Kate leaned back into her seat and breathed in the moment. The lights on the oak tree shone beautifully up the trunk, with the café lights hanging like falling stars.

She peered up between the strands of lights and could see in the dark blanket beyond a familiar bright star. She held it in her sight and thought, *Thank you.* The star's light blinked as she squeezed Zach's hand tighter and thought that maybe she could believe in the miracle of everlasting love, after all.

⇒ Epilogue ⇐

Kate and Zach stood staring out at the rows
of vines in the vineyard. Their vineyard.
The sun was just beginning to set over the lush
green leaves shading the clumps of fruit growing
larger each day. They would finally be harvesting their own yield this season.

Kate reached down and picked up the pot
that held the rosebush and placed it next to one
of the end posts. The bright red roses shivered
in the light wind and seemed to glow against
the green of the vines.

Zach put his arm around her shoulders, and she rested her head against his chest. The sunlight played delicately against each surface as the hues turned from yellow to orange.

Kate realized in that moment she was happier than she had been in a long time. Looking up at Zach, she said simply, "I love you."

He squeezed her shoulder and then looked down with his beautiful blue eyes and planted a sweet soft kiss firmly on her opened lips.

"I love you, too."

They continued to watch the sun setting on the vines, and Kate realized that she didn't need to plan ahead to figure things out. For once, she could trust that it would happen exactly the way it should.

Letter from the Author

Dear Reader,

Thank you for joining me again on the Texas wine trail! When I first wrote *Cactus Christmas*, book #1, during the pandemic at the end of 2020, I never really thought I would be embarking on a series. Yet, as the story began to enfold, and the more time I spent researching in Fredericksburg, I found myself wanting the story to continue. I wasn't the only one! Many readers finished the book quickly and messaged me asking when the next one would arrive.

It was a tight turnaround to publish this in time for the wedding and bluebonnet season in the Hill Country, but I felt that was only appropriate considering the theme. Thank you for taking the time to read, and share! I look forward to meeting you between these pages again this fall when Cactus Cradle, book #3, comes out!

Until then, please come support the local businesses and wineries highlighted in my books. I hope to see you on the Texas wine trail, very soon!

Warmest wishes,

Heather

Locations visited on the

Texas Wine Trail

Open Air RV Resort
Spicewood, TX
www.openairrv.com

Vaudeville
Fredericksburg, TX
www.vaudeville-living.com

Blue Bonnet Café
Marble Falls, TX
www.bluebonnetcafe.net

The Ragtime Oriole
Marble Falls, TX
www.theragtimeoriole.com

Otto's German Bistro
Fredericksburg, TX
www.ottosfbg.com

Jack Allen's Kitchen
Austin, TX
www.jackallenskitchen.com

Kerrville Hills Winery
Kerrville, TX
www.kerrvillehillswinery.com

Stonewall Motor Lodge
Stonewall, TX
www.stonewallmotorlodge.com

Limestone Charm RV Park
Fredericksburg, TX
www.fredericksburgtxrvpark.com

Texas Heritage Vineyard
Fredericksburg, TX
www.texasheritagevineyard.com

Alamo Springs Café
Fredericksburg, TX
www.alamospringscafetx.com

Pontotoc Vineyard Weingarten
Fredericksburg, TX
www.pontotocvineyard.com

Navajo Grill
Fredericksburg, TX
www.navajogrill.com

Wildseed Farms
Fredericksburg, TX
www.wildseedfarms.com

The Liquid Culture
Fredericksburg, TX
www.instagram.com/the_liquid_culture

Ab Astris Winery
Stonewall, TX
www.abastriswinery.com

Locations visited in Pacific Northwest

Next Door Gastropub
Port Angeles, WA
www.nextdoorgastropub.com

Bourbon West
Port Angeles, WA
www.facebook.com/bourbonwest

Crescent Beach RV
Port Angeles, WA
www.crescentbeachrv.com

For more information:

texaswinetrail.com
www.wineroad290.com
www.visitfredericksburgtx.com

⇒ Acknowledgements ⇐

I have many people to thank for helping this series continue:

Thank you to Dan, and the team at NYBookEditors. Megan McKeever, I am so grateful that you were able to provide your expertise and guidance for my line/structural edits again. You asked me to dig deeper, and I hope I did you, and the characters, justice. I know that the book is better for it! Thank you, Alison Imbriaco for your detailed comments and suggestions on my copy edits. You really helped fine-tune my words to present a cleaner, more palatable, story.

Christine, you knocked it out of the park again with this amazing cover! Thank you for caring enough to put all the extra effort and details into making this book gorgeous. Victoria, thank you again for your beautiful illustrations. I know the readers love them just as much as I do.

Thank you, IndieReader, for providing a wonderful space for independent authors and publishers to share their work with a wider audience.

Cindy Davie, always my first-pass reader, I can't thank you enough for your feedback and support (I'll buy the guacamole, anytime!). Thank you, Diane Hussey DeChillo, for continuing to read my manuscripts and providing timely and meaningful feedback. Thank you, cousin Caitlin McCown, I love your insightful comments, and enthusiastic encouragement. Thank you, Jill Harper Andrews, for keeping me in check with my architectural references.

Thank you, Susan and Billy Johnson of Texas Heritage Vineyard. From the real bottling incident to welcoming me into the THV family. I am grateful to have your input and support, and I'd gladly "baptize" my Tecovas boots at your vineyard anytime. Thank you, Tyler Buddemeyer, for answering all my questions, texts, and phone calls about the winemaking and viticultural process.

Thank you, Chris Brundrett of William Chris Vineyards. The phone call we had helped illuminate so much of the business of Texas wine-making for me, and gave me inspiration that I will continue to draw on as I work on book #3. Thank you for all you do to champion 100% Texas wine.

Thanks goes out to the wineries who continue to support and help me share my books; Perla at Messina Hof (Fredericksburg), Perry at Los

Pinos Ranch Vineyards, and Deanna at Long-horn Cellars.

Thank you Jeff Cope at Texas Wine Lover, for sharing my books with your readers. Andrew Klein, I'm grateful that you continue to want to read and review my books with such thoughtful consideration!

To my family, I am grateful for you support and encouragement! You ground myself in the belief that these words come from the true source, and I can trust they will do the work of healing, en-couraging, and giving hope as they are meant to.

To my greatest champion, who gives the sweet-est kisses, shakes her goat tail until her little butt seems like it will fall off, and who always is there to listen to my plot twists and turns: Dotty. I love you more than words can ever express and I couldn't do this without you.

Finally, to YOU, my readers. Thank you for letting me share this continuing story of hope, faith, love, and Texas wine! I love my small book club groups, house meetings, and getting to know all of you along the way. Stories are meant to share, and I thank you for sharing mine lovingly with others.

Raise a glass, and let's toast to this 2nd book! I'll see you back on the trail as I continue to "research" and write book #3.

CACTUS CHRISTMAS

A TEXAS WINE TRAIL SERIES

⇒ BOOK 1 ⇐

Heather Renée May

ORDER TODAY!

Find out where you can order online, or pick up signed copies at participating wineries on the Texas wine trail!

heatherreneemay.com/books

CACTUS CRADLE

A TEXAS WINE TRAIL SERIES

⇛ BOOK 3 ⇚

Heather Renée May

COMING IN 2022!

Sign up today for email notifications of pre-sale, book tour events, author meet & greets, and much more!

heatherreneemay.com/subscribe

About the Author

HEATHER RENÉE MAY is passionate about fourth quarter pivots, and delighted she can finally channel her love of wine into something productive. She works as a software engineer, plays music at wineries and breweries (Heather Ré), and lives full-time in an RV with her sweet rescue pup, Dotty. They split their time between the Hill Country of Texas, and the Pacific Northwest. You can find out more on her website: www.heatherreneemay.com

Made in the USA
Coppell, TX
30 March 2024